The McCoys of Holy Rock

What Others Say About Books by Shelia E. Bell

"Shelia E. Lipsey is one of the few authors who sets my heart to blaze with her writing. Her writing is intense, complex, unforgettable and most of all, needed in the world today. Shelia's novels have everything Christian fiction novels need: brilliant plots, timely conversations, and faith building passages! Keep your eyes on Shelia E. Lipsey...she is definitely a legend in the making." --- Ella Curry, president of EDC Creations. Publisher of Black Pearls Magazine. Based on novels Beautiful Ugly and My Son's Wife

By Sherri Gregory March 27, 2016 "The Real Housewives of Adverse City)
Shelia, you have done it again, your writing style, storyline and great details as always is above and beyond . From page one to the end, I was talking to myself and turning the page to see what are they going to do next? I got into each character individually and as couples, the drama and life situations are here and there is a lot! Everybody has a separate journey, and I can't wait to see how they handle this. Shelia, please come on with the next book. I can't give anything away (as bad as I want to, especially Pastor Carlton Porter- he is all over the place and he is spreading more than the gospel around). but I can tell you this please get your copy, I'm telling everybody I know this is a must read, you will enjoy.

The Life of Payne by Shelia E. Bell This book was clearly a tall tale of struggle, Payne and how much can one endure the hardships from as close as a family member as your mother. No matter what the main character did to earn her love, he still was pushed away. Sadly, this fictional story is all to real for many individuals that have family members that are addicted to drugs or just blatantly lost their way. Shelia Bell knows how to flesh out the most from her characters so that she can deliver the best to her readers. Superb job, looking forward to reading more from this author. Amazon Reviewed by Michael D. Beckford, Author of "Little Black Bird"

The McCoys

of

Holy Rock

by

Shelia E. Bell

The McCoys of Holy Rock
Copyright 2017 © Shelia E. Bell

ISBN: 978-1-944643-02-7

Library of Congress Control Number: 2017909287

Cover designed by Rebecca Marie - thefinalwrap.com

Dedication

To all the literary supporters who have made this series of characters come alive and stay alive, forcing me to keep moving in my God given talents and gifts.

Acknowledgements

This is dedicated to the ones I love, the ones who continue to push me to do what I have been called to do. I thank God for blessing me with the gift to imagine. I thank Him for motivating me to keep going even when I have tried to talk myself out of doing what I know I have been chosen to do, which is write. I thank Him for placing the right people along my path and removing the wrong people out of my way so I can keep pressing forward. I am eternally grateful to each reader, to every bookclub that supports my work. I'm always thankful and grateful to my family and friends. Thank you Lacricia for never saying no when it comes to editing my work. Thank you to Regina Dobbins because she is my Robinette and the best beta reader around. I can go on and on but I will stop now so you can get to reading about "The McCoys of Holy Rock!" They are about to set the church on fire!

Love y'all so much

Shelia E. Bell

The sign outside of Holy Rock

Holy Rock Ministries
40th Jubilee Celebration

1

"There are three things in life...not worrying what they are, not caring what others may think they are, and enjoying the wonder of what they might be." Tom Althouse

Senior Pastor Hezekiah McCoy and First Lady Fancy McCoy relaxed in first class on their return flight from Paris, France. It was the third extravagant trip they'd taken in the past year. Before Paris, the couple enjoyed a twelve-day Alaskan cruise, and before that, they joined a pastor and wife from another church on a trip to Cozumel, Mexico.

"Can you believe that changing our identity has never come back to bite us? I mean it's approaching five years since we relocated to Memphis, and we haven't had a single issue. I felt a little shaky when we applied for our passports, but bingo, no problem at all," Fancy smiled and squeezed her husband's hand.

"Look, Fancy, no need to bring that up," Hezekiah said in a soft tone to assure that the passengers around him couldn't hear him. "That's why I shelled out plenty of money for our new identities. I'm just glad we had cash stashed away so that when we got out of prison we could afford to get the best of the best. Dude covered all the bases for us."

"You're right. I mean from new birth certificates, social security cards, passports, the whole nine yards. It's like we entered into a witness protection program because our past has been totally eradicated." Fancy laughed lightly.

"Like they say, you get what you pay for. And for us, it gave us a new chance at life." This time he squeezed Fancy's hand and kissed her on her right temple.

"Yeah, the price wasn't cheap; it left us with nothing, but for us to become Hezekiah and Fancy McCoy, it was worth it. And the boys, well, I'm glad we were able to legally change their last names instead of having to do it the way that we did ours."

"Fa sho, baby. Fa sho."

Fancy leaned over in the plush first class seat, resting her head on Hezekiah's shoulder. "Baby, do you think we travel too much?"

Hezekiah looked at his wife, shook his head and sighed. "Okay, now where is *this* coming from? You always have to have something to worry about, Fancy. What would make you say something like that?"

"I don't know. I was just thinking. I mean, I know you're the senior pastor at Holy Rock, but before we left for Paris, I heard grumblings from some of the members."

"Grumbling? What kind of grumbling, and from who?"

"Some of the members have been talking about how much time you spend away from the church and the pulpit."

Hezekiah eased around, readjusted himself in the seat and looked into his wife's eyes. "I don't care what anybody says. Let them come to me with that bull and I'll set 'em straight. I've been the senior pastor of Holy Rock for two years. Before that, I was the associate pastor. You, of all people, know that I've given my all to that church, and so have you. I won't let anyone make me feel guilty about indulging my wife or my family. You hear me?"

"I'm just saying. I don't want a lot of unnecessary drama started. Don't get me wrong; I love the way you spoil me with all of these exquisite trips. I love the jewelry you lavish on me too," she said as she looked on her wrist at the expensive diamond encrusted timepiece. "But I don't want folks looking upside my head like they have a problem with the blessed life God has allowed us to live."

"Look, I may not rake in the millions like some of those pastors on television, at least not yet," Hezekiah smiled, "but Holy Rock treats me nice, real nice. You know what I mean?"

"Yes, baby, I know exactly what you mean."

"And hey, the church membership has grown almost triple since I became the senior pastor, so there's no need to worry your pretty little self about a thing. Remember, you were worried when we moved out of the house Stiles turned over to us when he left Holy Rock. But what did I tell you about that?"

"You said we deserved to have our own and not something already lived in."

"Exactly. Now don't get me wrong, it was a blessing when we were able to move from a cramped apartment and into that house, but it's nothing like choosing our own. And the icing on the cake is that the church pays for it all without us having to do anything wrong."

Fancy shifted her head slightly and then said, "You're right. It's just that you know how some folks can be, baby. That's all I'm saying."

"And like I said, I'll handle anyone who tries to stir up mess. We're going to enjoy our lives as much as we can and as often as we can. So enough of that talk. Now what about the boys. Have you talked to them?"

"Yes, I called them before we boarded the plane. They're fine. Khalil was actually at church when we talked, which nowadays is the norm for him, praise God. He was going over the plans for the senior youth participation in Jubilee. I can't believe it's just two weeks away."

"Neither can I. How did he say that's coming along?"

"He says everything is going according to plan," Fancy responded. "And if that's what he says, then that's what I believe. He's committed to what he does. Who would have thought that he would come out of that juvenile detention center a totally changed young man. No more drugs. Can you believe God delivered our son from heroin and coke? Baby, it's a blessing."

"Yes, God is a good God. And our youngest? I assume Xavier was somewhere with his head buried in an African American history book of some sort, huh or on that game?" Hezekiah remarked, his thick lips upturned slightly to form a smile.

"You know it. He said he was at home reading a book called "Eyes Off The Prize." At least, I think that's what he said it was called. Something about the United Nations and the African American struggle. Later he and Raymone are supposed to be going to the movies."

Hezekiah's chest seemed to poke out a little, listening to Fancy talk about their two sons. His oldest son, Khalil's life had taken a total turn for the better after he was released from a boys' juvenile detention center in Chicago. Initially, when it was time for his release, he was dead set against moving to Memphis with his parents, but when his maternal grandmother suffered a heart attack, he had no choice. In order to be released he had to have someone sign papers stating that he would live with them and that person or persons would be primarily responsible for him. Fancy's father, the boys' grandpa, told Fancy and Hezekiah that a troubled young adult living in the house would be too much on his ailing wife, especially with Khalil's drug abuse and criminal history. So, he really had no choice and within days after his release, he relocated to Memphis where he began to flourish. He spent a majority of his time at Holy Rock working with youth and young adults, much like his mother used to do at the church.

Hezekiah saw the positive change in his son and he was grateful. Khalil seemed to love the church, and it didn't take long for Hezekiah to appoint him as the Youth Ministries Director. The young man loved his new role and proved to be quite good at it. He thrived beyond Hezekiah and Fancy's wildest imagination. It was definitely an answered prayer.

Their youngest son, Xavier, who had never given them a moment's trouble a day in his life, was still the same Xavier; smart as a whip and enthralled in learning all about the struggles, history, and religion of African Americans. He had an insatiable love for gaming, too. Unlike his brother, who changed girlfriends like he changed underwear, seventeen year old Xavier was more of a loner. He was quiet and reserved and other than hanging out with his best friend, Raymone, he kept to himself.

Overall, life for the McCoys was pretty darned good, which was why Hezekiah didn't want anything tarnishing what he had built for himself and his family. He would address Fancy's concerns about meddling, gossiping church folk as soon as he got home. That was for sure.

2

In every marriage more than a week old, there are grounds for divorce. The trick is to find, and continue to find, grounds for marriage. Robert Anderson

Rena gathered the last few items of clothing and toiletries and placed them in her carry-on luggage bag while Robert stood in the doorway, his arms crossed, and a deep furrow on his brow. His bearded face revealed it had been some time since he shaved, something he used to be obsessed with doing. Lately, things had been on shaky ground for him and Rena.

"So how long are you going to be gone *this* time?"

"What do you mean by that?" A deep wrinkle stretched across her own brow as she spoke. Her voice escalating in an unpleasant tone, she continued. "Look, I don't know what you're insinuating, but the last I checked I was not your slave, Robert. I'm your wife. So get over the attitude already."

"Attitude? I wouldn't call it that. I'm just sick of you running to Memphis to that dang church every time you hear about something going on there. What is it about that place, Rena? You would think that after five years together and four kids that you would be over dude."

"Is that what you think this is about? Or should I say is that *who* you think this is about? Stiles? Get over it, Robert. It's Holy Rock's fortieth Jubilee, and I don't see one reason why I shouldn't be able to go to Memphis with my parents to celebrate it without you making a stink over it. Mom and Dad aren't getting any younger, you know, and I don't see why you have a problem with me traveling with them."

"Have it your way," Robert shrugged his shoulders, turned around, and walked away.

"Uhhhh," Rena said aloud.

Her text notification sounded, temporarily distracting her from what had just happened between her and Robert.

"You ready sweetheart?" her mother texted.

"Yes, you and dad otw?"

" be there shortly."

"K. See you in a few," Rena replied.

"Bye," her mother responded.

Rena finished the last of her packing and then hurried to the family room to tell the kids goodbye. She was determined not to let Robert dampen her mood or rob her of her joy. She parked her luggage at the front door then went to the family room where she saw the kids piled up on the sofa watching a movie on Netflix.

"Make room for Mommy," she told one of the kids.

Rena looked at the faces of each of her four kids. Two though she hadn't given birth to, were just as much hers as the twins who she conceived with Robert. They were the four reasons she continued to fight for her marriage to survive. Granted, lately she may not have been fighting as hard as she probably could have, but nonetheless she was in the fight to win.

For the past year, she and Robert's relationship seemed to hit one brick wall after another. Rena didn't know if it was the routine of their relationship, their up and down financial situation, or if it was the fact that she felt like Robert's feelings had changed somewhere along the way. Initially, when she noticed the change in him, she thought it had to be another woman but she soon dismissed that thought. Robert was not the cheating kind. At least Rena didn't believe that he was.

Shelia E. Bell

The fact that he was so upset that she was going to Memphis for the weekend with her parents was almost too much for her to take. She wouldn't describe Robert as a jealous man, but ever since she and Robert met and fell in love, Stiles had been the thorn in Robert's side. Robert told Rena and her parents on numerous occasions throughout the years that Rena had never gotten over her feelings for her ex. Rena couldn't understand that thought process because as far as she was concerned, Stiles was nothing but a distant memory from a painful, long ago past. Sure, she was concerned about him and his family and probably always would be, but that was the extent of it. After all, before Robert, Stiles was not only the first, but he was the only man, she had ever slept with or fallen in love with, so of course it would stand to reason that he would hold a tender spot in her heart, but nothing more. If Robert couldn't see after all the years they'd been together that she loved him, then that was his problem. She had enough day-to-day worries dealing with the kids and her career.

Mr. and Mrs. Jackson arrived, came inside, and said their hellos and goodbyes to their son-in-law and their grandkids. Rena followed suit by kissing and hugging her children, forewarning each of them to be on their best behavior for their father while she was away.

Robert walked them to the door, barely saying two words.

"I love you. I'll see you Monday," Rena told him and kissed him on his cheek.

"Enjoy yourself," he said dryly, as he waited for her to exit the front door after which he abruptly closed it.

Rena shook her head, pursed her lips, and walked toward her parents' car. She couldn't hold back the excitement swelling inside at the thought of getting away from Massachusetts, if only for a few days.

‡

Stiles wasn't particularly looking forward to his trip to Memphis. His emotional wounds and pain remained fresh. Since leaving Memphis after the death of Baby Audrey two years ago he hadn't returned to the city. The thought of returning to Memphis and to Holy Rock only served as a cruel reminder of the devastation he experienced there. Losing his little girl because of the stupidity of his lying, cheating, ex-wife, Detria, made his anger fester until he could hardly manage to get through each day. Several of his newfound church friends tried to tell him that holding on to his grief in the manner in which he was doing, was not good for him. But how could they know if they never experienced losing a child, an only child at that. People could say what they wanted to say, but Stiles didn't care. He couldn't let go of the anguish inside no matter how hard he tried and how much he prayed. The thought of Detria and how she ruined his life was ever present.

His friend and confidante back in Memphis, Leo, was the one to tell him that Detria's baby daddy and Stiles' former friend, Skip, was still married to Meaghan. Meaghan was the girl Skip was sleeping around with while he was seeing Detria. Skip and Meaghan had a baby of their own, too and with all the money Detria had shelled out to him when she got her high seven figure settlement from the car accident, Skip opened several Subway franchises, and was doing quite well for himself.

Elijah, the little boy he had with Detria, lived with him most of the time. Detria never really cared much for children, which was obvious when Baby Audrey was alive and now evident with her son. Stiles had heard that she hadn't put up much of a fight to keep him from Skip once she got over the initial fact that he was married and had moved on with his life. On the contrary, she had fully recovered from the tragic accident and except for limited mobility in her right arm, she was back to the old slick, conniving, selfish Detria.

Stiles chuckled lightly to himself as he thought about how she had all of that money but probably no peace. He packed his last few items and said aloud, "Vengeance is mine, saith the Lord."

3

A secret's worth depends on the people from whom it must be kept. Carlos Zafon

Nervously rubbing her left arm and breathing heavily, the mysterious woman waltzed through the airport terminal like she was a jet setting millionaire. Her stride revealed confidence and she had a certain air of sophistication about herself as she prepared to board her flight to Memphis.

She'd been silent for forty-one years, forty-one years too long. Now was the time for her to step out of the closet, show her face, claim her place, and shock the Grahams, especially Pastor. Her sister, being the mean conniving control freak she was, had played her, taken advantage of her illness, and like a fool she had allowed her to do it. The witch had forced her to keep her silence back then by threatening to tell everyone about her illness. But now there was no longer a reason to hide because the wicked old witch was dead.

As she approached the airport boarding ramp, the woman carried on a conversation with herself. "Chauncey Graham, I'm going to show you that I'm not one to play with. And while I'm there, it will be the perfect time to pay my dear sweet boys a visit. Certainly, they'll be glad to see me." A disturbed look engulfed her round, full cherub-like face as she thought, *This visit to Memphis is going to be good. It's going to be real good.*

‡

Pastor was elated that he was going to render a message during the Jubilee service. It had been years since he'd graced the pulpit and delivered a Word from the Lord. Accepting Hezekiah's offer to share a word gave him a sense of renewed energy. To think that once again, God had shown him favor to the point that he felt like his old self again was incredible. Two strokes, the death of his soulmate, Audrey, the secrets that had been unearthed after her death, and of course the tragic death of his granddaughter, Baby Audrey, were all enough to crush a man's spirit and make him question his trust and faith in God. But not Pastor. He held strong to his faith and refused to believe that God had forsaken him. His wife, Josie, was in good health too and for a couple who had both recently celebrated seventy years on earth, they were living quite well. They travelled occasionally and entertained frequently.

Speaking on Jubilee Sunday wasn't the extent of Hezekiah's generosity. He had recently asked Pastor to return to Holy Rock as one of the five associate ministers he had on staff, and again, Pastor humbly accepted the role. He would oversee the Seniors' Ministry. He and Josie already taught a senior's class on Sunday mornings. It was something he'd always wanted to do with Audrey, but Audrey had always been into being a trophy wife and a showpiece for Pastor. As for Josie, she loved teaching just as much as she loved God. She had served in the church all of her life and had been a Sunday School teacher for years up until the year she fell and broke her hip. She was incapacitated for quite some time but when she met Pastor, she was on the mend and back to being the vibrant Josie she once was.

Josie was right by Pastor's side, supporting him, helping him with his study notes, and similar to Audrey, she kept her man dressed sharp. They made a good couple.

"Honey, I printed your notes for Sunday School and your speech for Sunday."

Pastor walked over to Josie and planted a kiss on her cheek. "Thank you, baby."

"I guess we'll do some shopping later today. I want to find something special to wear for Jubilee. And you could use a new suit yourself," Josie told Pastor as she stood up from the computer and faced him.

"Nothing to it, but to do it," Pastor jovially said. "We can have lunch while we're out. How about that?"

"Okay, I'd like that. I've been wanting to try that new Italian restaurant in midtown."

"Anything you want," Pastor said, patting Josie on her rear and kissing her again, this time on the lips and with deep affection.

As they got dressed and ready to go out, they talked about Hezekiah and Fancy. "What do you think about Pastor McCoy's expensive taste?" Josie asked Pastor. "Some of the senior ladies, who attend the Golden Friends monthly luncheon, say that he and the first lady spend far too much time away from the church. They say when you were senior pastor, and even when Stiles was pastor, that neither of you believed in gallivanting around like him and First Lady Fancy."

"That's none of our business, and what people need to keep in mind is that everyone is different. None of us are the same. Pastor McCoy and Sister Fancy happen to love exploring new places. That's on them."

"I guess so," Josie said hesitantly. "But the trips are so lavish, and it's not like he's going on these trips because he has to speak at other churches. He and Fancy seem to be travelling the world on the church's dime. I'm just telling you what folks are saying."

"Are you sure you don't feel the same way these *folks* feel?" Pastor questioned.

"I just think that they both should be more considerate of the church's expenses and what people say."

"And I say, if they *are* taking advantage of the church and its benefits, then that's between them and God. God will bring to the light anything that's not of him."

"You always say that, Pastor."

"I say it because it's true. Let God handle it. We're here to serve Him and trust in Him. Now to change the subject; I can't wait to see my children. Stiles should be arriving Friday morning and if Francesca and Tim decide to come they'll drive down early Sunday morning."

"I'm so glad that you and Francesca talked. It's an answered prayer. And her health, she's doing well, isn't she?"

"Well, we've only spoken a couple of times over the last few months, but she did call last week to tell me that they might drive down for Jubilee."

"That's still good for Francesca. You know she shuts herself off from you and Stiles so whenever she does decide to reach out, it's a blessing. That's all I'm saying."

"Yes, you're right, and God is good. For someone with AIDS, Francesca defies the odds every day. No one but God can do that. No one but God."

"Well, are you ready to go?" asked Josie.

"Yes, I'm ready."

They locked up the house and walked out into the two-car garage. Pastor proceeded to walk spryly toward his black on black Lincoln Continental.

"Honey, I think we should go in the Mini Cooper. You know how difficult it can be finding a parking space downtown, and at least with the Mini we can ease into the smallest of parking spaces."

"You're right," Pastor said. "The Mini it is." He opened the door to the green and black, four door Mini Cooper and waited for Josie to get inside before closing her door and walking around to the driver's side.

"Babe, do you think Stiles is bringing his new girlfriend with him?" Josie asked, as they headed to their destination.

"He didn't say anything about bringing anyone with him. And according to him, he's not involved with anyone. He says he and that woman I think you're talking about, uhhh, I can't call her name right now, are friends. Her daddy was the pastor up until he died. She works at the church," Pastor replied.

"Yeah, I remember you saying that her daddy died and that she works at the church. I'm just glad to hear Stiles laughing again. When I talked to him last week, he sounded like the Stiles I knew before his divorce and before, well you know, before poor little Baby Audrey died." Josie's sadness resonated in the tone of her voice and the expression on her face.

"Yes, he's come a long way," Pastor added. "And he still has a long way to go. But all I can do is trust that in time God will heal his heart totally and completely."

"Enough of that. I'm just excited about Jubilee. I know the church is going to be packed; if that's even possible since it's almost always at overcapacity on Sundays already."

"That's one thing I can give Pastor McCoy credit for; he knows how to draw the people to the church. He has some powerful, life altering sermons. I'm sure he's going to deliver another one on Jubilee Sunday."

"I'm sure he will," Josie said.

4

*"The truth is, unless you let go, unless you forgive
yourself, unless you forgive the situation,
unless you realize that the situation is over,
you cannot move forward."* Unknown

Stiles was scheduled to fly out on a red eye Friday morning, but Tuesday evening after Bible Study, he went online and cancelled his flight. He decided to drive the eight and half hours from Houston to Memphis. He believed it would help to relax his mind. He would listen to his motivational audio books, play some of his favorite music, and spend some alone time with God.

He contemplated asking Kareena to come along, but changed his mind about that, too. He really liked her. She was sweet, sensitive, and his definition of sexy. When he was with her, he felt at peace, not stressed, but calm and satisfied. That was the reason he had to steer clear of the two of them embarking on a relationship other than friendship. He didn't want to hurt her and he didn't want to be hurt again either. He wouldn't even take it to the good Lord in prayer, because he didn't want to chance God giving him the approval to become involved with her.

Kareena was not only sweet, she was kind, generous, a great listener, and she loved the Lord. Stiles felt that she understood him and she definitely didn't judge him. She didn't pressure him to be in a relationship with her, but they did spend lots of time together. Being one of the daughters of the late pastor of Full of Grace Ministries, Kareena knew everything there was about the ministry. When Stiles accepted the pastoral position at the small church, he asked Kareena and another one of her sisters to remain on board as members of his ministerial staff. Kareena was the church administrator. Her oldest sister and her sister's husband were the youth ministers.

Under Stiles' leadership, the church membership began to see some growth. God was blessing the ground where Stiles treaded and for that he was grateful.

He thought about his baby girl often. He missed her smile, her chubby cheeks, and her awesome daddy hugs. As for Detria, he hadn't spoken to her since the divorce. She had tried reaching out to him a few times after he left Memphis, but he ignored her calls and deleted her messages, then decided the best thing to do was to block her number from his phone.

He hoped he wasn't making a mistake by agreeing to attend Holy Rock's Jubilee service and the banquet they were having on the eve of Jubilee. Understanding that Pastor was expecting him to be there, Stiles was glad that Pastor was back to a version of his former self. His father was healthier than he'd been in quite some time, had clarity of mind, and was still happily married. God had restored what the locusts stole and Pastor was involved with the ministry of Holy Rock, the church he loved. So Stiles understood that it was essential that he be there.

Stiles called Francesca and she told him that she and Tim might drive down, but she wasn't one hundred percent certain. He sure hoped that she would come down because he missed her. He hadn't seen his sister in a couple of years, and it wasn't like she or Tim were on social media.

Stiles arrived home from Bible Study, and soon as he stepped into the 1,700 square feet house that the church leased for him, he went inside his man cave, plopped down on the leather sofa, propped up his feet, and grabbed the remote to change to First Take. He watched it until he started dozing off.

"Guess I better get in the shower," he said aloud when he awoke from a light, short sleep. His cell phone rang just as he stood up to head to his bedroom.

"Hey, what's up, Kareena?"

"Do I need to put a tracker on you?"

Stiles laughed. "What are you talking about?"

"You mean to tell me that you drove all the way home without missing your wallet? I went into your office to leave that printout you asked me to drop off and there it was, on the floor by your desk."

"Dang, I sure didn't. I'll swing by there tomorrow. Did you put it up for me?"

"Actually, I didn't. I just brought it with me. You said you weren't coming back until Monday, so since we don't live that far from each other, I thought I'd drop it off."

"I hate that you have to go through all that trouble."

"It's no trouble and what else do you propose, Stiles? You know you need your wallet and you can't drive around town, let alone out of the state, without it. I'll be there in a few minutes."

"Thanks, Kareena. I'll be on the lookout for you."

Stiles and Kareena had one sexual encounter a few months after they initially met. That's another thing that led Stiles to try to keep things casual between him and Kareena. If he wasn't careful, he could see himself possibly falling in love with her. She was just that special to him, but love was not for him. That was proven after two divorces and two deceitful ex-wives. He and Kareena both had talked about it, but like him, she agreed they were better off as friends.

The man Kareena once loved deeply was Carson Peele, her high school sweetheart. Carson's family attended Full of Grace Ministries too, so like Kareena, he grew up at Full of Grace. He was active in the high school JROTC program so almost immediately, after he graduated from high school, he went to the Army and Kareena left Houston to attend Jarvis College in Hawkins, Texas.

The young couple remained faithful to each other while pursuing their life dreams. Less than a year after completing basic training, he received orders that he would be deployed to Afghanistan. He was granted a short leave before deployment. Carson returned home, asked Kareena for her hand in marriage, which she gladly said, "Yes." They made plans to become husband and wife after he completed his tour but unfortunately, the marriage never happened. An Army hummer he was riding in ran over an undetected land mine. Carson, along with four other soldiers, was killed. So, Kareena and Stiles both had their stories of tragedy and they both wanted to shield their hearts.

The night he and Kareena crossed the line, their desire for each other was at an all-time high. They had gone out for dinner one evening after Sunday church service. They laughed, talked, and reminisced about their past loves, the highs and lows of life, and how loneliness crept into their otherwise routine life every now and then. Stiles drove her home that evening, walked Kareena to the door, and without planning to, he kissed her goodnight. They couldn't deny the passion ignited between them. Staring into each other's eyes, words did not need to be spoken. Kareena's hands trembled as she tried to unlock the side door to her house. She was so nervous that she dropped the key. Stiles picked it up, unlocked the door, and led her inside. That night, the flesh definitely proved weak. They didn't plan to fornicate; they desired to live lives pleasing to God, but on this night, their passion, their desire, their loneliness, and their flesh said otherwise.

Stiles spent the night lying next to Kareena. The following morning when they woke up, she prepared a light breakfast and coffee for the two of them. While they enjoyed breakfast outside on her small patio, they talked and vowed to remain friends, but promised each other that they would not venture down that path of love and lust again.

Now here they were, Kareena was outside, about to come into his house and Stiles secretly wished things could be different. When he went to the door to watch for her, Kareena was already out of her car and walking toward the front door.

"Here you go," Kareena said, walking up to him and pulling his wallet from out of her purse. "Tie this around your neck if you need to. You do not need to be driving on the highway without it and I do not want to get a call to come bail you out of jail," she fussed playfully.

"Yes, ma'am. Maybe I need to take you along; that way I know I'll have everything I need," he innocently flirted.

"We both know that's not a good idea," she quickly shot back.

"You want to come in, have a cup of coffee, tea, a glass of wine?" he offered.

"I don't think so. I'm beat. It's been a long day. You know how Tuesdays are at Full of Grace. Meetings all day, Bible Study, evening worship service. I'll talk to you before you leave. When do you think you'll be leaving since you decided to drive instead of fly?"

"I don't know. I haven't made up my mind. I have my class to teach at the community college tomorrow evening so I still might leave early Friday. As long as I'm there for the banquet Saturday evening, I'll be fine. Look, seriously, why don't you ride with me? You said you've never been to Memphis. There may not be a whole lot to see, especially since the weekend will be filled with activities at Holy Rock, but you could at least see the church where I used to pastor and I could use the company."

"Are you sure that's the only reason or do you want me to come along so I can help you drive?" she quipped, still standing inside the door to Stiles' house.

"Now that you mentioned it, that's not a bad idea." The both of them laughed. "Seriously, I should have asked you before now. Please come to Memphis with me. I promise to be a good boy and bring you back home safely."

"I don't know. It's such late notice. And you said there's a banquet Saturday evening. That means I have to have something fancy to wear. You know I like the more casual look so I don't think I'll fit in. Maybe next time."

"Look, go home and sleep on it before you make a final decision. I thought I was ready to go face my demons alone, but the more I think about returning to Holy Rock, to Memphis period, the more I'm having second thoughts about even going."

"Okay, I'll think about it."

"Thanks, Kareena. I don't know what I'd do without you."

"Believe me, you'll be just fine, Stiles. Goodnight."

"Goodnight. And thanks again for bringing my wallet." Stiles stood at the door and watched until Kareena got in her car and drove off. His flesh awakened as the light hypnotic trace of her body scent lingered inside his door.

Kareena drove to the end of Stiles' driveway and out of his view. She tapped on the brakes, bringing the car to a complete stop before she put it in PARK. She needed a moment to gather her thoughts and bring her flesh back under subjection. Her heart skipped a beat as she thought about Stiles' tall, handsome frame. He reminded her so much of Carson. His forgetfulness, his smile, his gentle spirit....his kiss. Everything about him reminded her of just how much she missed Carson.

"Why, God? Why did you let Satan take Carson away?" she prayed. "Why? We would have had a wonderful and perfect life together. I just know it. By now we probably would have a family. We would have been so happy." Kareena gripped the steering wheel and laid her head against it for several seconds before telling herself to leave. She didn't want to chance Stiles seeing her parked at the end of his driveway like she was a stalker chick.

"Pull yourself together," she chastised herself. She turned the key to start the car, put it in drive, and drove home with tears cascading down her face like a waterfall.

5

No man is rich enough to buy back his past. Oscar Wilde

Pastor awoke suddenly, turned over onto his right side, and for a moment, he imagined Audrey was lying in the bed next to him. It took only a second or two for his mind to connect with his vision to see that side of the bed was empty. He looked to the left of him. He picked up his cell phone from the nightstand next to the bed—8:36 PM. He hadn't meant to sleep this late. He had spent most of his day at Holy Rock, which had become custom for him since he was now part of the paid ministerial staff.

When he arrived home, it was five o'clock in the evening. He had a sandwich and then told Josie he was going to lie down and take a power nap until it was time for dinner. During his sleep, he dreamed about Audrey. It didn't happen often. Usually when he dreamed about her, he felt she was trying to tell him something. That was Audrey though. Seemed like dead or alive she kept up with everything and everybody at Holy Rock. Pastor rose from the bed, swung his legs down to meet the floor, and smiled at the thought that even up in heaven with God, she was still making it her business to intertwine herself with him here on earth.

In his dream, she was talking and pacing across the floor, dressed like she was going to walk the runway for one of those top name designer fashion shows. Suddenly, Pastor stopped smiling, and a troubled look washed over his face as he tried to recall something in the dream that disturbed him. He couldn't put it together, but he felt a dis-ease in his spirit.

"So you finally decided to get up, huh? I thought you were out for the night. You must have had a lot on your plate at Holy Rock today," Josie said as she appeared in the doorway and walked into their bedroom.

"Yep, you know there's a lot going on around there in preparation for Jubilee. Pastor McCoy wants everything to go perfectly. Several pastors and their wives and families are flying in, along with three guest choirs. And then you know the banquet is Saturday night."

"Yeah, the weekend will be here before we know it. I still need to go look for a pair of shoes tomorrow to go with the dress I found. I guess I'll call Millie and see if she wants to go with me.

Millie was a dear friend who Josie met at a Golden Friends event. After talking at length with Millie, Josie found out that she lived in Emerald Estates too.

Pastor and Josie had moved back to the house in Emerald Estates after Pastor's health improved. Josie didn't have a problem with it. It may have been the house Pastor once shared with Audrey Graham, but Josie wasn't bothered. Let the dead rest in peace and let the living keep living until they die. That was one of Josie's sayings.

Millie moved to the neighborhood when her son and his family purchased a home one street over from Pastor and Josie. The two women spent a lot of time together, primarily going shopping or out for lunch.

Pastor stretched and yawned, but didn't move from off the bed.

"Are you still tired?" asked Josie.

"To be honest, I definitely *could* go back to sleep," Pastor replied and chuckled lightly. "But I need to take a shower and now that I'm sitting here, I feel myself getting a little hungry."

"Why don't you go ahead and take your shower. I'll fix you a plate by the time I think you're done," Josie offered.

"That sounds good. What'd you cook? Not that it matters, cause everything you make is good enough for a five star restaurant," he said.

"I bet you tell all your women that," Josie came back, giggling. "Fried pork chops, collards, cornbread, fried corn, and mashed sweet potatoes. I made a gallon of sweet tea with lemons, too."

Sounds delicious. Anything for dessert?" Pastor loved to indulge in his desserts from time to time. When Audrey was alive, he tried to steer clear of them because Audrey developed diabetes and he didn't want to, in any way, tempt her to eat unhealthy.

"I made a pan of frosted chocolate brownies."

"Yum. You know you know the way to my heart."

"Man, take your shower so you can eat your dinner and so I can do like you just finished doing - go to bed."

"You don't have to tell me twice." Pastor got up and undressed down to his boxers before heading to the bathroom. As he showered, he hummed one of his favorite songs, *You Ain't Seen Your Best Days Yet*, by Bishop Paul Morton. He hummed and sung until the memory that he'd dreamed about Audrey took precedence over his thoughts of the song. Once again, an unexplainable uneasiness settled over him. *Audrey, I miss you, honey. Not a day goes by that I don't think of you.*

In his mind, as the warm jets of water streamed down his body, Pastor thought of all the years he was with his dear Audrey. All the good times and the not so good times. He thought about the day he saw Audrey waltz into Holy Rock, holding the hand of her little boy, Stiles. She was a vision of beauty. He shook his head briefly from side to side like he was trying to toss a memory from his mind. He opened his eyes as he simultaneously rubbed both hands over his face to brush away the heavy stream of water. One memory after another came and went.

Then there was one memory etched in his mind that he didn't want to think about; hoped he could forget but couldn't. It was the memory of the woman he once loved before Audrey. There was a time he thought she would be the one that he would spend the rest of his life with. But after being in and out of her life for two years, he came to the realization that something was not quite right. It took some doing, but he was finally able to completely break things off with her. Thank God that he did, because it paved the way for his heart to receive the love of Audrey.

Pastor tried to suppress the unpleasant memories of the woman, but every now and then they reared their ugly head. Today was one of those times. My, my, my, if only some things could stay hidden forever.

6

Do not judge my story by the chapter you walked in on.
Unknown

Fancy curled up on the plush sofa in her and Hezekiah's bedroom to relax and go over the menu and program for the banquet, which was three days away. As for the banquet committee, Fancy understood that they would say that it was too late to make any drastic changes, but then again, if there was anything she saw that she didn't like or that was missing, she was going to make sure that the banquet committee made the changes regardless. She wanted everything to be perfect and was determined to make it so. Not only that, but for the first time since they moved to Memphis, Hezekiah's aunt was coming to town this weekend. She would see firsthand how the two of them had grown in the ministry. Their lives, much like their oldest son, Khalil, had been transformed only by the grace of God. No more illegal shenanigans. They were enjoying the fruits of their labor and God was truly rewarding them for their diligence and service.

The fact that his aunt called and told him that she was coming to Memphis this weekend filled Hezekiah with an extra dose of joy. Fancy was happy for him, too. She had always shown Fancy nothing but kindness ever since her and Hezekiah became a couple. The woman would be arriving tomorrow morning. Hezekiah and Fancy were going to pick her up from the airport. Fancy had already made sure that one of the guest bedrooms was fixed up perfectly for her stay. Fancy's parents weren't going to be able to attend but they sent a special love offering for the occasion.

Hezekiah always said that his aunt was super nice. Growing up, he didn't see her often, but when he did, she always came bearing gifts. When his father was gunned down in the streets near Cabrini Green projects, it was his aunt who came to be by his mother's side. She made sure that Hezekiah and his older brother were fed and taken care of, allowing Hezekiah's mother time to grieve over her husband's death. Then when his mother died while he was in prison, Hezekiah didn't think he would ever be able to forgive himself for being locked away while his mother was at home dying. Again, his aunt helped him through the most difficult days of his grief. She came to see him almost every visiting day and encouraged him, talked to him, and soothed his hurting heart as much as she could through prison bars. She kept money on his books while he was locked up and sent him letters and books through the mail. She even offered to take care of Khalil and Xavier when Hezekiah and Fancy went to prison but Fancy's parents interceded and provided for the boys' care.

A light tap on the door roused Fancy. "Yes?" she answered softly.

"Mom, it's me."

"Oh, come on in."

Her oldest son, Khalil, entered. "Hey, Mom."

"Hi, Khalil. You're home early aren't you?" She picked up her cell phone and looked at the time.

"Yeah, I left church a little earlier than usual. I came to scoop up Xavier."

"Oh, okay. Where are you two headed?"

"The bowling alley. We're meeting a few friends from church and hanging out."

"That's nice. I wish you weren't moving out," Fancy said, quickly changing the subject. "I don't understand why you feel that you need to do that," she complained.

Khalil wasn't in the frame of mind to hear his mother grumbling about his decision to cop his own crib. Ever since he told his parents that he had found an apartment and would be moving the week following Jubilee, his mom had been riding him about it. "Mom, I'll be twenty-one in a couple of weeks. I have a great position at Holy Rock that I love and that pays me well. So why wouldn't I want to move into my own spot? I'm a grown man."

"Because, Khalil, you have all the freedom you need right here. One of the reasons your father and I decided to move into this big house was so you and Xavier would have plenty of space and we wouldn't be on top of each other. Now you want to just up and move out?"

"Come on, you know it's not like that. I mean, this will always be home. But this is yours and dad's place."

"You just want to bring some of those hot tail girls from Holy Rock to your place. I told you all they want is to hook up with the pastor's son. They want the glory and the title of being your wife." Fancy huffed. "You better think with more than what's below your belt, son."

"Hey, you ready to vamp, bruh?" Xavier appeared in the doorway.

"Yeah, I'm ready. Mom, we'll talk later," Khalil said, glad for his brother's perfect timing. He walked over and stood above Fancy, leaned down, and kissed her on top of her hair.

"Y'all be careful out there," Fancy said to her sons.

"See ya later, Mom," Xavier said as he and Khalil turned and walked out of the room.

‡

"Thanks for being my alibi," Xavier told his brother as they climbed in Khalil's Lexus LC 500 coupe. The off-the-showroom floor candy apple red ride was an early birthday present from his father.

"No problem, but you know sooner or later you're going to have to come clean about what's going on with you. I'm your brother, your only brother at that. I've made my share of bad decisions, so I don't think it's much of anything you can tell me that would make me surprised or judgmental, you know?"

Xavier side glanced his brother as Khalil drove out of the driveway and pulled out into the street. "Yeah, I know, but it's nothing to tell. I just wanna hang out with my friends sometimes. I'm almost grown, a senior in high school, but Mom still treats me like a kid. I have a car that she hardly ever lets me drive. And the handful of times that she does let me drive, I can't be gone but a couple of hours. And Dad says nothing; he lets her get away with it. Mane, what's up with that? I can't wait until I graduate and turn eighteen next year."

"You know how mom is so you're just going to have to learn to deal with it for a little longer. I'll be moving into my spot next week. You know you can always come hang out. Remember that."

"Yeah, that'll be cool. Thanks, bro."

"I gotcha," Khalil said.

Satisfied with his brother's offer and feeling more at ease now that he was out of the house, Xavier put his earbuds in and started listening to his long playlist of songs on his iPhone.

Khalil drove out of their gated community and headed towards downtown. It took less than twenty minutes to arrive at Raymone's house located in Harbor Town. Khalil didn't really know much about Raymone, except that he and Xavier were good friends and he attended Holy Rock Upper School, the same as Xavier. Xavier had plans to go to the movie later on and meet up with some more friends. Afterwards, Raymone was going to drop Xavier off at home. Hopefully, their parents would be asleep when he got there.

"Thanks, again," Xavier told his brother when they made it to Raymone's as he got out of the car.

"Text me if you need me to come back and scoop you up."

"Sure thing," Xavier told him as he turned to walk down the pathway leading to Raymone's front door.

"Y'all be safe. You got protection on ya, right? These females can be treacherous out here," Khalil said, sounding half-serious and half-joking.

"Always," Xavier assured him and chuckled. Throwing up his right hand, he approached the front door and pushed the doorbell while Khalil drove off.

7

*But in the end she is as bitter as poison...*Proverbs 5:4a

Khalil and a group of young people from Holy Rock bowled several games, with Khalil's team losing. Khalil sat around at the end of the last game. A couple of the girls flirted with him, which he was used to. He wasn't into any of them but he wouldn't deny that he had shared the bed with quite a few females from Holy Rock, not to mention girls from around other places. He was a good looking guy if you asked the women. His smooth, deep dark melanin skin, flashing smile, and charming personality wooed the ladies.

His mom was wrong when she told him he had all the freedom he needed at home. That was quite the lie. From time to time he sneaked females in the house, which was easy to do because the five thousand square foot house simplified things for him. He also had access to a one-bedroom casita that was on their three-acre property. The only time it was in use was when his parents had a number of guests at the house. His father had caught him a time or two when he was entertaining females in the casita, but Hezekiah basically gave his son the thumbs up when he saw that Khalil was occupied. Having his own spot would alleviate any unwelcomed guests or embarrassing interruptions. He didn't have to do anything but move his clothes and other personal belongings into the fully furnished one bedroom loft he found in downtown Memphis. The loft had a spectacular view of the mighty Mississippi. He couldn't wait to pick up his keys next week and move in.

Khalil tuned out the girl sitting next to him whispering in his ear and zeroed in on an attractive, somewhat older looking female a few lanes down from where he was situated. When he was a teenager and heavy into the streets and drugs, he messed off with a few older women. He found them more to his liking because they seemed to be more grounded, realistic and not all hung up on getting married or pregnant. The ones he bedded had a little cheddar and helped support his drug habit. He didn't miss being involved with drugs and crime, but he did miss the perks that came along with being involved with an older woman.

Khalil was glad, with the help of his parents, that the drug and crime fueled life he lived as a teen was behind him. He was thankful that he had wised up enough to get clean and sober. He never wanted to go back down that path again. He often shared his story with teens at church, especially during the teen summits his mother implemented at Holy Rock when she worked with youth. It felt good being sort of a mentor for younger people.

When his father first talked to him about sharing his testimony of deliverance with other young people, Khalil balked at the idea. He was far from being a speaker unless it was to talk up on some drugs. But, much like Hezekiah, he had the charm and charisma to captivate an audience.

Hezekiah kept pressuring Khalil to talk to the youth and Khalil kept bucking against the idea, until one Thursday evening, during a teen summit for at risk youth and adolescents, after constant prodding from his mother, he reluctantly approached the podium and began sharing his story. When he finished and went to take his seat, the auditorium full of young people stood on their feet awarding him with a standing ovation. Khalil felt invigorated at that moment and was pleased that perhaps he had helped to make a positive difference in someone's life. It was also at that moment that Hezekiah felt the prompting of the Holy Spirit to place Khalil in the position of assistant youth director. It was a decision that Hezekiah had not regretted. Within a year of being off drugs, and living in Memphis, Khalil had made a complete about face.

When his father promoted him to Youth Director of Holy Rock a few months ago, Khalil knew that it was nothing short of a miracle for his life to be as magnificent as it was now. He smiled as he reverted his thoughts to the mysterious woman at the end of the lane. Slightly pushing off the girl who had been all up in his ear, Khalil excused himself and walked toward the woman when he saw her get up and go to the food court by herself. *Game on,* he thought.

Khalil increased his pace when he saw her retrieve her beverage from the automated dispenser, turn around, start walking with it…and then drop it. One hand rose in frustration mid-air, a menacing frown instantly replaced the tempting smile he'd seen minutes earlier.

After three, maybe four, giant leap-like steps, Khalil was at her side offering his assistance. "Let me help you with that."

She looked at him and her smile accentuated her large, perfectly made up brown eyes and arched brows. The lady didn't object to Khalil's offer. "Thank you," she said, her voice soft but less confident than he would have imagined.

"What was in your cup?" Khalil asked.

"Sugar free lemonade."

"Sugar free lemonade, huh. Yeah, I'm sure you're plenty sweet already. I'll be right back." Khalil walked past her, went to the restaurant counter, and informed one of the restaurant employees about the mishap. He returned shortly, thereafter, with another lemonade. "Here you go," he offered, extending the cup toward her.

She received it with a smile. "Thank you again. That was so nice of you. My name is Dee."

"I'm Khalil," he countered. "Anytime, Dee."

8

The only people I owe my loyalty to are those who never made me question theirs. Unknown

Francesca continued to keep to herself, not bothering to communicate with Stiles and Pastor on a regular basis. Her and Tim's lives had been far too hectic, especially over the past year. Her health continued to yoyo. For the past few weeks, however, she had been feeling pretty good. She and Tim talked about making the trip to Memphis, and they both felt she would be able to make the short trip without incident.

She and Tim had been quite busy preparing the last round of adoption paperwork. Through prayer, GoFundMe, and their church family, their prayers about adopting a child seemed to finally be materializing.

This was the second time they'd gone through the adoption process. The first time they were denied solely on the basis of Francesca's diagnosis. Tim pushed Francesca not to give up just because they'd been rejected one time. He found a lawyer who was an expert in the area of fighting for the rights of people with disabilities and who had connections with international adoption. He pointed out to Francesca and Tim that the Americans with Disabilities Act was passed to insure that those with disabilities were not discriminated against. In regard to those with AIDS/HIV the law protected individuals with HIV whether asymptomatic or symptomatic.

It was a long battle, but Francesca gained more strength at each round of the fight, and now they were about to celebrate a true milestone victory, according to their lawyer. Everything looked favorable and in a few weeks they hoped to receive positive news about getting a child.

Francesca looked forward to attending Holy Rock's Jubilee service. This was when she planned to share the good news with Pastor and Stiles. Later that Thursday evening, she called her brother and told him she and Tim had decided to come to Memphis, but she didn't want him to tell Pastor.

When Francesca was young, she and Stiles had a good brother and sister relationship. It wasn't until he came home from divinity school and became involved with Rena, that things changed. But since then and since his divorce from Rena, and the death of his mother and most devastating, the death of his child, their relationship was slowly evolving. Though they still didn't talk much, he realized how valuable family, health, and life was and it was not to be taken for granted. So what if Rena and Francesca had a lesbian relationship. It happened before he and Rena got together, and it was a choice the two of them had made. Who was he to judge anyone? Did he agree with it? Definitely not. Did he believe it was a sin? He most certainly did, but so was fornicating and he'd done plenty of that. The more he grew in the Lord, the more he realized that there was not a big sin and a little sin. Sin was sin. He had to let go of the unforgiveness if he was going to move forward in his life. He prayed that the time and day would come when he could stand before Rena and tell her how sorry he was for the way he treated her. He wasn't exactly a nice person back then.

Kareena seemed to be responsible a lot for Stiles' new outlook on life. She was so easy to talk to, and he found himself confiding in her some of his deepest, darkest secrets. It felt good to release the pinned up emotions he wrestled with. He had friends like Leo to call up and talk to, but it was nothing like Kareena. She had that certain, nonjudgmental way about her that made the words pour out of him. He suggested to her on more than one occasion that she should return to school and study to be a psychologist because she was just that good at listening.

"Pastor is going to be thrilled to see you and Tim," Stiles said to his sister when she told him their plans.

"We won't be able to come to the banquet, but we plan to be there in time for the second service," she explained to Stiles. "We'll hang out with you and Pastor for a couple of hours after service before returning home."

"Oh, yeah, they're combining all three services Sunday. They're just going to have the ten forty-five service."

"Okay, cool. I'll let Tim know. How are things going on your end? Are you still enjoying living in Houston and your new pastorship at Full of Grace?"

"Houston is huge and the streets are always crowded. You can't go anywhere it seems without getting on the interstate. As for Full of Grace, it's nothing like pastoring at Holy Rock. It's a much smaller congregation, but it's growing so I'm not complaining. I do miss the hustle and bustle of a church the size of Holy Rock, but it is what it is.

"Anybody special in your life?" Francesca prodded.

"No, I can't say that there is. I have friends and there is one special friend, but that's it. Nothing intimate," he told his sister.

"You deserve to love again and to be loved, Stiles. Don't shut love out of your life and out of your heart. If it can happen for me, I know darn well it can happen for you."

"Yeah, anyway," he said, disregarding what she'd said. "I can't wait to see you, Sis. We'll talk later. I need to concentrate on this road. I should be in Memphis in about three hours."

"Okay, drive safely. See you Sunday."
"Sure thing. Bye now."
"Goodbye, Stiles."

‡

Stiles turned up the volume in the car and jammed to a Bruno Mars song on his drive to Memphis. He wasn't able to convince Kareena to come along, but he couldn't blame her. He shouldn't have waited until the last minute to invite her. But maybe it was best this way. He needed to face the music in Memphis for himself. He was already feeling some trepidation about the visit, but Jubilee was extremely important to Pastor, especially since he would be speaking.

Pastor's renewed involvement in the church made Stiles feel extra proud and happy for Pastor. Hezekiah had proved that he respected the great work Pastor did in the past to put Holy Rock on the map. It said a lot for the church to still be flourishing after 40 years.

Stiles and Hezekiah spoke periodically via social media and phone from time to time. Initially, there was a rough patch between them when Hezekiah first took Stiles' place as senior pastor. Hezekiah fired all of the staff and brought in his own select people, including deacons and trustees. From what Stiles had heard, Hezekiah had also added himself as one of the authorized signees on Holy Rock's bank accounts. This was something Stiles and Pastor refused to do. They sat in on financial meetings and had valuable input of how the church's funds were to be spent, but they drew the line at being authorized signees. They never wanted it said that they had say so over the church funds because it would put them in a vulnerable position to be accused of too many illegal activities when it came to money.

Obviously, Hezekiah didn't share in that belief or practice. Once Stiles got over the way Hezekiah chose to run things, he and Hezekiah were cordial and cool. It touched Stiles deeply that Hezekiah gave Pastor a position at Holy Rock. Pastor was back to his old self because he was eager to answer the calling of God once again.

Stiles' phone rang. He turned down the volume of the radio before he pushed the button on the steering wheel to answer Kareena, whose name appeared on the dash.

"Hi, there," she said. "How is the drive so far?"

"Other than running into some major construction about 50 miles back, everything is good. That's basically the only thing that slowed me down. How are you?"

"I'm good. I'm home and about to sit down, watch my recordings on my DVR, while I eat. I was just checking in on you."

"That is very thoughtful of you. I still wish you had come with me."

"You'll be fine. Enjoy your family and seeing your friends and some of your former flock. I've been praying for you and will continue to do so. God's got you," she reassured him.

"You know," Stiles paused.

"What?" Kareena responded.

"You know you're a good friend," he said. "I thank God for you, Kareena. I really do. I'll call or text you when I make it to the hotel."

"Oh, so you're not staying with your father and his wife?"

"I thought about it, but decided against it. I think it's better if I stay at a hotel. I got a good rate for a four star hotel in east Memphis. It's close to the interstate, so I can jump on 240 and be at Holy Rock in fifteen minutes tops."

"Oh, well, I don't understand why you wouldn't stay with them. But you know better than I do. I'll let you concentrate on driving. I'll talk to you later. Drive safely."

"Will do. Bye, Kareena."

"Buh-bye," she replied.

Stiles disconnected the call and smiled as he turned the volume back up and continued listening to his playlist.

He practiced in his mind what he would say to Rena if she happened to show up at the banquet or at church Sunday. He had no reason to think that she would travel from Massachusetts for Holy Rock's anniversary, but he felt that her parents would. Knowing Rena the way he thought he did, she wouldn't let them travel alone if she could help it. If she didn't come and they did, he would ask them how she was only for curiosity's sake. He hoped that things with her and Robert were going well. Rena was a great girl. It was just they were younger and he couldn't swallow the fact that she had been his sister's lover and had contracted an STD from her that she didn't tell him about. It was too much at the time for his marriage to survive. Now that he was a bit older, and hopefully wiser, he could sincerely wish her the best. He was still full of anger when she used to reach out to him. When she called to extend her condolences for his little girl's death, he couldn't accept it. He was rude to her and now he wanted the chance to ask her to forgive him. There were many times he started to send her a message on social media or text her, or call her, but he talked himself out of it every time. This time, if she came, and if she gave him the time of day, he was going to be a man and talk to her. He wanted all of the bad blood between them to be washed away for good. If only he felt that way about Detria—but he didn't. He was still a work in progress. Being a man of God was one thing; being a man in the flesh was an entirely different matter. God still had a lot of work to perform on him, that much he knew for sure.

He continued his drive to Memphis. The next song that started on his playlist, "It Didn't Prevail" by Jason White and New Day, fit him and his situation to a tee. It was another one of his favorites. He listened carefully to the words and then began to sing along, *"Through every hurt, with every scar, it didn't prevail cause God is with me..."*

9

There are two ways to be fooled; one is to believe what isn't true. The other is to refuse to accept what is true.
S. Kierkegaard

Hezekiah sat in his home office going over his message for Sunday. Everything was going right in his life and for that, he was especially grateful. He had a fat bank account, a couple of nice rides parked inside his three-car garage, a beautiful wife who loved him deeply and a church full of dedicated and committed members who loved presenting him with 'love offerings.'

Jubilee would probably bring in at least a hundred thousand and that wouldn't include the money he stood to receive personally from many of his members. He didn't take a salary. Instead, he preferred a love offering, which was raised for him every Sunday and could easily tally five figures. Along with the love offerings plus all the extra perks he received from Holy Rock, one could easily surmise that Pastor Hezekiah McCoy was sitting on top of the world. He wasn't an Osteen, Jakes, or Dollar but he was definitely doing well for himself and his family.

Not that he needed to, but because he could, he had his hands in a little of this and a little of that at the church, but he didn't think it was enough to cause suspicion. He'd learned from his past and knew how to avoid getting caught with his hand in the church cookie jar. Only one thing, or one person, could mess things up for him, and that was his head of Security, George Reeves.

About a year ago, George started attending Holy Rock with his wife, Bernice. She was a faithful member while George only attended to keep peace at home.

During one of his visits, he thought that he recognized the McCoys from somewhere other than Holy Rock. It wouldn't have raised suspicion because the McCoys quickly became known not only at Holy Rock but in the mid-south community. But George's recognition went further than that. He thought there was something worth looking into with the dynamic duo.

Hezekiah leaned back in his office chair, placed the top of his ink pen to his lips, and inwardly cursed the fact that George was a sickening, nagging thorn in his flesh. He remembered that Sunday like it just happened yesterday. He had preached all three services and his voice had dwindled down to almost nothing. Yet, right before the end of service he left out of the sanctuary went to take a quick shower, customary for him, before he changed into the extra set of clothes he maintained in his church office. He planned to return to the sanctuary to greet his members as they exited.

This particular Sunday, after he'd performed his ritual and was about to go back into the sanctuary, he stepped outside his office and was confronted by a stocky, short white guy who looked eerily familiar. Hezekiah looked around. His armor bearers were nowhere to be found, and after what transpired, Hezekiah fired them. "Horace? Horace McKellar," the stranger said.

Hezekiah stopped dead in his tracks and stared at the man. He looked around again for his armor bearers. No one but him and this stranger were in the hall. Holy Rock was a diverse congregation but there was something that stood out like a sore thumb with this guy.

"I beg your pardon?" Hezekiah replied to the man. What did you call me?"

"I said, Horace McKellar. That is your name, isn't it?"

"I'm sorry. You're mistaken. I'm Pastor Hezekiah McCoy. Look, if you need help, you can go to the front

44

receptionist area and they can get one of the ministers to talk to you. Follow me. I'll show you," Hezekiah said, trying to hide the nervousness in his voice. Who was this man? How did he know his real name? This could not be good for Hezekiah. He continued to walk down the hall, hoping to run into his armor bearers, and get this dude escorted out of the church. But was that what he really wanted. With this man knowing who he was, it may not be such a good idea.

"I think it's time we had a little one on one," the man said. "If you talk to me now, I don't see why I would need to bring the first lady into this."

Before Hezekiah could respond, one of his armor bearers appeared. Hezekiah looked at the armor bearer with anger in his eyes. His nostrils flared and he balled his hands into a tight fist like he was trying to keep himself from bursting.

The armor bearer must have detected the look on Hezekiah's face and realized that something was not quite right. "How can I help you, sir?" the armor bearer asked as he walked up on the man.

"You can't help me," George said. "Pastor McKel, uh, Pastor McCoy, will you tell him that you and I go a long way back, and we're just catching up?"

Hezekiah thought that he'd better see where this dude was coming from and what, if anything, he knew about him and Fancy. "Yeah, we do. Look, give us a few minutes. Tell one of the associate ministers to greet the congregation."

"Pastor, are you sure about this?" the armor bearer asked, as a second armor bearer walked up.

"Everything okay?" this one asked.

"Everything is fine. This is an old friend of mine. I haven't seen him since..."

"Since he moved from Chicago to Memphis," the man interrupted, causing Hezekiah to swallow deeply.

"That's right. It's been a minute. Anyway, we're going to be in my office," he told both armor bearers.

"Sure. I'll stay here outside your door," the first one said.

"We won't be long," Hezekiah told the armor bearers.

"Yes, Pastor. I'll go let Minister Eddie know that you won't return to the sanctuary," the other one said.

Hezekiah turned and went back to his office with the man who knew too much following behind him.

That day changed everything for Hezekiah as he listened to the retired Chicago police officer tell him that his name was George Reeves. George explained how he and his wife had relocated to Memphis from the Chicago area after he retired from a position in felony law enforcement. They wanted to be closer to their daughter and grandchildren. He was not a churchgoing man and did not consider himself to be religious, but his wife was just the opposite. She rarely missed a Sunday going to church, and ironically had chosen to join Holy Rock and insisted that he come along. To appease her and keep his home life in check, he frequently accompanied her. *Happy wife, happy life*, he told himself.

His "cop intuition' kicked in and he began to make it his personal mission to delve deeper into the McCoy's past, seeing that he couldn't shake the feeling that the couple had something to hide. He didn't forget a face easily, and he had an uneasy feeling about this so called 'man of God.' He already distrusted men of the cloth, seeing them only as wolves dressed in sheep's clothing. Listening to the sermon that fateful morning only added to his philosophy that all preachers were no more than hustlers, trying to get over. It became his personal mission to find out just how much of a hustler this

Hezekiah McCoy was, and if there was something he was hiding. What he uncovered was enough for George to confidently approach Hezekiah and tell him what he knew about him and Fancy. He threatened to spill the beans to the congregation and anyone else who would listen about Hezekiah and Fancy's past unless the two of them could perhaps come to an agreeable compromise.

If George snitched, it stood to chance that it would ruin everything Hezekiah was finally building up in his life.

Their meeting that Sunday boiled down to the two of them having several long and heated meetings. Hezekiah agreed to bring George on as head of Security. He paid him a nice salary, plus extra money under the table, all for George to keep his mouth shut. Part of their arrangement was that George was not to approach Fancy with any of what he knew about the felony couple and their past. George had no problem agreeing to Hezekiah's terms, as long as the dollar bills continued to flow his way.

To this day, Hezekiah had maintained his word and George upheld his end of the bargain. Other than the fact that George was just as crooked as Hezekiah, the man looked out for his investment, *Hezekiah and Fancy McCoy*, as if his very livelihood depended on keeping them and their secrets safe - because it did.

10

Time moves in one direction; memory in another.
W. Gibson

Saturday evening arrived and the fall weather
presented perfectly clear skies, billowy clouds, and the
temperature hovered in the seventies with a gentle breeze.

Hezekiah and Fancy, who some members jokingly
called the *Marjorie and Steve Harvey* of the Christian
world, because of their over the top fashion statements
and extravagant lifestyle, stepped inside Holy Rock's
newly built 12,000 feet multipurpose hall. Hezekiah's
head was raised upward like he was King of the jungle.
As far as he was concerned, he *was* the king of Holy
Rock, Fancy his queen, and their two sons, heirs to the
throne.

The first family didn't go directly into the banquet
hall, but instead were whisked off by George and
members of his security team to a private area of the hall
that had a number of smaller breakout rooms for more
intimate events and gatherings. The plan was for the first
family to remain out of sight until Pastor welcomed the
guests, prayed, and then Minister Eddie would introduce
them. They would come out and onto the purple carpet
that was rolled across the glossy floor just for their
entrance.

Inside, the banquet hall was exquisite with a drapery
entrance, soft amber uplighting, and an amber tint
washing over the glossy floor. Guests entering could be
seen and heard relaying their utmost satisfaction of the
setup and decorations. Each clothed table was surrounded
by eight clothed chairs, with fresh bouquets of fall
flowers, and place settings that sparkled as if they had

bits of diamonds encrusted in them. There was a complete staff to welcome guests and direct them to their pre-assigned tables. Everything was perfectly placed.

Fancy and Hezekiah relaxed while they viewed everything taking place inside the hall from closed circuit television. Fancy couldn't be happier with the way things appeared. It reminded her of one of the beautiful Paris halls she and Stiles had been blessed to visit.

Some of the mid-south's top political heads and officials, along with prominent pastors and their first ladies were in attendance.

Rena and her parents, Mr. and Mrs. Jackson, entered the luxurious hall. She gasped at its beauty, as did her mother, as they were escorted to their table. Rena took her seat and wasted no time people watching. She recognized some of the long time members as they made their entrance.

Mr. and Mrs. Jackson got up from the table to go mingle with old friends who they hadn't seen since leaving Memphis. Rena remained at the table alone, glancing around, fake smiling as strangers passed her by, and taking in the splendor of it all. *Pastor McCoy has really made his mark on this city*, she thought to herself. *It looks like the entire city of Memphis is here. I wonder if Stiles is coming.*

Continuing to look around, she smiled when she caught a glimpse of Pastor at the front of the room. He looked like he was headed toward the stage area. Someone announced that the banquet was about to officially start.

The escorts brought two couples to her table. Rena didn't know them, but they exchanged pleasantries and smiled at each other as the couples sat down.

Visually searching for her parents, Rena saw them standing several tables away talking to some other guests. She got up and headed in their direction to let them know that the banquet should be starting and they probably should return to their table.

Moments after they returned to their table and sat down, Pastor walked up to the podium and began talking.

"I want to welcome everyone to the fortieth Jubilee of Holy Rock. God is good and we are blessed. I'm thankful to be standing here, able to see somewhat clearly," he laughed lightly, "all of you beautiful people who have come to celebrate this joyous occasion. Please stand and join me for prayer."

Pastor proceeded to pray and when he was done, departed the podium. Rena followed him with her eyes and saw him sit down at a full table. Her tummy fluttered nervously when she spotted Stiles.

Minister Eddie walked up three steps leading to the stage and approached the podium. "Those who are able please remain standing to welcome the First Family of Holy Rock," he announced.

A thunderous round of applause filled the room. Rena turned to the side and looked toward the back of the room to watch as the First Family entered.

Hezekiah looked handsome in a black designer tuxedo with all the manly trimmings. Holding her hand, Fancy walked beside him looking radiant in a custom designed royal purple, tiered, peplum dress that rested just slightly above her knees. Dripping from her neck, wrist, and hands was a girl's best friend—diamonds. Khalil, Xavier, and Hezekiah's aunt, all just as fashionably dressed, followed.

The applause continued as the first family nodded at the guests and walked up the aisle leading to the front of the room.

Since she was standing, Rena was able to gain a clearer view of Stiles. He stood next to Pastor, looking handsome as ever in a black tailored suit. Rena felt her tummy do a somersault.

As the first family drew closer to their table at the front of the room, Pastor's eyes widened. Josie stood to the right of him. He took hold of her hand like he needed to steady himself. It didn't seem to be enough so on the other side of him he latched onto his son's arm and held on.

Stiles looked down at his father, and in turn helped to steady him. "Are you all right?" Stiles leaned in and whispered.

Barely able to speak, he slowly nodded and responded weakly, "Yes. I'm...I'm okay."

"What's wrong? You look pale," Josie whispered in his ear with a concerned look on her face and in the tone of her voice.

"Nothing," he whispered. "Just felt a little dizzy for a second. I think I got up too fast. I'm good now."

"Ladies and gentleman, the McCoys of Holy Rock," Minister Eddie announced again.

Like royalty, Hezekiah and Fancy waved and then the family took their respective seats.

"You may all be seated," the minister instructed the crowd after the McCoys sat down.

Pastor, still wobbly and shaken, sat down. Beads of sweat formed on his forehead. He removed his white handkerchief from his pocket and wiped his brow.

"Are you sure you're all right?" First Josie then Stiles asked.

He reassured each of them that he was fine, all without taking his eyes off the woman who looked identical to someone from his past. Someone he wanted to forget.

11

Sometimes we are taken into troubled waters not to drown but to be cleansed. L. Daskell

The program portion of the banquet was complete with entertainment that included a gospel band, praise dancers, and presentations. Politicians and pastors alike came forward to praise Hezekiah for the outstanding job he was doing as the senior pastor of Holy Rock. A couple of them acknowledged Pastor and Stiles for their past positions. Each person who came up and spoke presented Hezekiah with an envelope as they passed his table.

"Pastor, look at Pastor McCoy's table. See that woman sitting at the table with them?"

"Yeah, what about her?"

"Doesn't she remind you a little of mother?" Stiles said casually while indulging in the first course of a three-course meal.

Pastor coughed into his handkerchief. "Umm, no not to me." He picked up the glass of water in front of him and took a swallow.

Hezekiah's aunt pushed back from the table and stood up. "Excuse me, I'm going to the ladies room," she told Fancy. "I'll be back shortly."

"Okay," Fancy replied and pointed. "It's over there, down the long hall, and to the right. Do you want me to go with you?"

"No, I'll find it."

Pastor watched as the rather short hippy woman got up from the McCoy's table. "Josie, I'll be back. I need to go to the men's room." He removed the napkin from his lap and placed it on the table, then stood up.

"Are you sure you're okay?" she asked him again.

Pastor tried not to show that he was somewhat anxious. Seeing the familiar looking woman had him jumbled up on the inside and confused in the head. If she was who he thought she was, what was she doing here? He hadn't seen her in years. It couldn't be her because if it was, how did she know the McCoys?

"I told you, I'm good, Josie. Now, I'll be back in a few," he said, sounding agitated.

"Hey, where are you going?" Stiles asked his father.

"To the can," he said. "I'll be back."

Entering the long hallway leading to the restrooms, Pastor saw people going up and down the hallway, in and out of doors, and in and out the bathrooms.

There she is. He started walking toward her as she was coming toward him.

"Hi, Chauncey. Long time no see," the woman said nonchalantly, while she walked up and kissed him lightly on his cheek.

Pastor's skin turned red as a beet when he saw her up close and heard her voice. "Margaret? Is that you?"

The woman laughed as if basking in the knowledge of the power she seemed to have over him at that moment. "Who else could it be, Chauncey? Surely, I haven't changed that much. Well, maybe a few extra pounds here, a couple of wrinkles there." Margaret pushed back loose strands of black hair from her face and laughed.

"What are you doing here?" He walked further down the hall, with her walking next to him, until they came to a room that was open and empty. Taking her by her elbow, he led her into the room and closed the door. Next, he turned to face her and stared at her baffled. "I haven't heard or seen you in….I thought you were…."

"Dead? You thought I was dead? Well, I'm not." She chuckled. "Far from it."

He gritted his teeth. "I asked you a question. What are you doing here?" he pronounced slowly.

Looking him up and down, a sudden icy contempt flashed in her eyes. "I don't answer to you, Chauncey. I'm not that young naïve, stupid, starry-eyed fool of a girl I used to be. Back then I was stupid in love with you until you showed me that you were nothing but a slick, two-timing dog. Anyway, aren't you glad to see me?" she said flippantly.

Pastor disregarded what she said and presented a question of his own. "How do you know the McCoys?"

"I know a lot of people. Does that make you nervous, Chauncey, or do you prefer that I call you Pastor like the rest of 'em?"

"Cut the shenanigans, Margaret and tell me what reason you have to be here? And what does it have to do with the McCoys?"

"First of all, it *is* Jubilee and I can be wherever I want to be. You don't have a thing to do with what I do or where I go. You made that clear when you dumped me and married that woman."

Pastor walked up, closing the small gap between him and Margaret, who was barely an inch shorter than him. Grabbing hold of both of her upper arms, a swift shadow of anger swept across his face as he spoke. "Look, I don't know what you're doing here or what you're up to, and frankly, I don't give a...."

"Whoa, watch your mouth there, *Pastor*," she said with emphasis. You *are* in God's house and you *are* supposed to be a man of God. I know you wouldn't want anyone to know that you have a nasty little old mouth now would you?" she countered icily. "We'll most definitely talk later." Margaret laughed, then turned, opened the door, and boldly walked out of the room, leaving a stunned Pastor standing with his mouth open and his eyes fire red with anger.

Pastor waited a few minutes before leaving out of the room and returning to his seat. When he entered back into the hall, Margaret was already seated. He watched her chattering with Fancy and some of the others at the table, still wondering who she was to the McCoys. One thing he was sure of, whatever the reason she was at Holy Rock, it couldn't be good.

The banquet continued without incident. Everyone appeared to be enjoying themselves and having a good time. As it approached the end, guests started getting up. Some mingled and others began to file out of the banquet hall and out to the parking lot to leave.

"It's good to see you." Rena, who was standing next to her table, turned around to see the person behind the voice she knew so well.

"Hi, Stiles. It's good to see you as well," she said rather politely.

"How's the family?" he asked.

"Good," Rena responded. "How are you?"

"I'm blessed." Stiles looked at Rena's parents who were still seated. He hugged and spoke to each of them and acknowledged the other guests at the table. They all exchanged light, friendly banter for the next several minutes until Stiles gently grabbed Rena by her elbow. "Can I talk to you for a few minutes? Preferably somewhere private."

She looked at him and as casually as she could manage, replied, "Sure." She looked at her parents. "Mom, Dad. I'll meet y'all outside."

"Okay, sweetheart. Stiles, it was good to see you," her mother said. "I've been praying for you and I'm going to keep praying for you and your family."

"Thank you, Mrs. Jackson. I hope to see y'all tomorrow. I just know the Holy Spirit is going to be all over the service tomorrow," he added.

"Yes indeed," Rena's father agreed, as did the others at the table.

Stiles and Rena pushed through the growing crowd of people, speaking to some, shaking hands with others, until finally after several minutes, they were outside in the parking lot. He led her to his car, unlocked it, and opened the door for her, beckoning her to get inside.

Rena looked puzzled and a little nervous, but she got inside, and Stiles closed her door.

When he got in the car, he exhaled then looked over at her. "You look good," he complimented. "Looks like life is treating you really well."

"Things *are* good," Rena replied forcefully.

"How's Robert."

"Robert's good."

"And the kids?"

"They're good," she said, not offering anything more.

"That's good to hear," Stiles responded.

"Look, let's cut through all the formalities. What's going on? I mean, the last few times I reached out to you to see how you were doing, you let me know without mincing words that I was the last person you wanted to talk to. You didn't seem like you could even stand to hear my voice. Now all of a sudden we're sitting here in your car, pretending like we're best buddies. I don't understand."

"I know you don't. And I'm sorry for all of that. I told myself that if by chance you came this weekend, I was going to make it my business to talk to you, to set the record straight."

"Set the record straight? What are you talking about?" She swallowed hard, lifted her chin, and boldly focused on him, thinking that he was about to say something else distasteful toward her.

"I'm talking about the way I've treated you when you've always been nothing but kind to me. You've showed your concern during everything I've gone through over the years. The death of my baby girl, well, let's just say, it left me in a bad way. God has surely put me through some fiery trials."

"But you're a strong man, Stiles." Rena's voice softened. "A strong man of God. I can only imagine what you've been going through, and I'm so sorry. That's all I was trying to tell you when I reached out to you."

"See, that's what I mean." His tone was apologetic. "You are always so kind, so positive. And me, I've been nothing but rude and unkind toward you. Rena, I just want to say that I'm sorry. I'm sorry for everything. I'm sorry that I treated you so badly during our marriage and the divorce. I'm sorry that I judged you when I have so many demons in my own closet. I'm sorry that I didn't see that you were only trying to be my friend when I was going through everything with Detria and losing my little girl, and even when my mother died. God has been dealing with me, you know."

Rena listened, too stunned to cry. She could feel her face become flushed. Her heartbeat picked up its pace, surprised by this unpredictable man.

"I don't know what else to say, but to beg you to forgive me. I know now that's what's been missing in my life—a lack of forgiveness. I can't move forward until I forgive, Rena. I had to start with you. I want you to know that I really did love you. You still have a piece of my heart. It's just that I couldn't accept what happened between you and Francesca."

"There's no need to apologize, Stiles. I understand. At least, I do now. I have to admit that I'm no angel either. I should have told you about Frankie and me…I mean Francesca. I should have told you about the STD. About everything before we got married, but I didn't. I was ashamed of what me and Francesca were doing. I felt trapped by her and sorry for her at the same time. I didn't know how to handle things. I'm sorry that I hurt you, Stiles. And for the record, I loved you too."

They sat in the car in silence, both looking straight ahead. A stream of people poured out of the hall. Many of them were laughing and talking as they went to their cars. Some stood on the parking lot talking.

"There my parents are," Rena said suddenly, pointing at the group of people walking in the direction of where Stiles was parked.

"Where?" he asked.

Rena continued pointing. "Right there," she said.

"Oh, yeah, I see 'em now. Well, I guess I better get back inside and catch up with Pastor and Josie. I want to talk to Pastor McCoy and his family, too."

Rena placed her hand on the door handle. "For what it's worth, thank you, Stiles. What you said means a lot. And I want you to know that I accept your apology, and I hope you'll forgive me, too."

"Forgive you for what?"

"For not being the wife and the woman you needed."

Stiles answered, "It wasn't you. It's just that it wasn't meant to be, Rena." He leaned over and kissed her on the cheek

Rena heard his quick intake of breath and a soft gasp escaped her. Trembling, she opened the door, put one foot outside the car, then turned and looked at Stiles. She spoke the next words carefully. "I think there's a part of me that will always love you." Rena hurriedly got out of the car and closed the door behind her without waiting for a response.

Stiles leaned back against his seat assailed by a terrible sense of guilt when he thought of how unfair he had treated the woman he once loved. As he watched her approach her parents, the heaviness he carried around all of these years slowly began to dissipate. He felt a sense of relief, felt lighthearted, like maybe he could finally move forward with his life. *Goodbye. You're the one that I let get away.*

"Where are you son?" The text from Pastor said.

Stiles opened the car door, got out of his car, and momentarily stood in the parking lot next to it. He looked around. Rena and her parents were no longer in sight. He texted his father. "Was outside, headed back in. Where are you?"

"Still inside. Can you take Josie home? Something came up and I need to meet with some of the ministers about tomorrow's service."

"Sure. She ready?"

"Yes. Meet you at entrance."

"Ok."

12

If you carry bricks from your old relationship to your new one, you will build the same house. Unknown

Pastor pulled around to the back entrance of Holy Rock and waited until he saw Margaret exit from the door that he told her to come to. He reached over and opened the passenger door as she walked up to his car.

"I feel like I'm going on a secret mission," Margaret teased as she climbed inside the car and closed the door.

"No time for jokes, Margaret." Pastor drove off the parking lot in a hurry. He didn't say another word to Margaret although she was going on and on about her excitement to be in Memphis. He continued driving until he arrived at a walking park located a few blocks from Holy Rock. Driving along the winding road, he entered the park, drove into a parking space, turned off the ignition, and looked at her with eyes that were hard and scornful.

Margaret looked around, surveying her surroundings. There were very few cars or people in the park. "I hope you didn't bring me out here to do away with me," she said, suddenly feeling uneasy but trying to sound calm and unbothered.

"You know darn well I'm not going to do anything to you, so stop with all the shenanigans. You were always so, so overdramatic. I want to know one thing, and don't give me another one of your smart answers. Tell me. What...are...you...doing here, Margaret? What do you want?"

"What kind of silly question is that? Anyway, I'm so proud of Hezekiah and Fancy. Aren't you? Oh, and to answer your question, I have some special news to share.

It's not the kind of news you want to share over the phone or FaceTime, you know."

"Share? Share with who? And you wouldn't know how to FaceTime anyone, so stop all of the buffoonery. I'm tired, Margaret. Enough with all this game playing."

Margaret stopped the sarcasm and suddenly her expression stilled and grew serious. "Look, first of all, you walked out on me—you left me, then the next thing I hear is that you're married. May the devil torture that woman's wicked soul! So, I don't think that gives you the right to demand anything from me. I'm in Memphis because I *want* to be in Memphis. I don't owe you any explanation other than that."

"Let me remind you of something, Margaret. I did not leave you for anybody. You're the one who left Memphis after you almost got me locked up. Calling the cops telling them I raped you just because I told you that it was over between us."

"You shouldn't have made me mad, and anyway, you didn't go to prison. I'm the one who got into trouble after I told them that I made the whole rape thing up. Don't you understand; you broke my heart, Chauncey? Things could have worked out if you hadn't married that woman."

"I will never forget what you did. As far as me getting married, you and I were done way before I met my wife. So leave it alone already and tell me what you're doing here." Pastor's voice escalated and he rubbed his forehead back and forth.

"That's a lie. Me and you were together for two years. Two years," she repeated with a raised voice and furrowed brow.

"Okay, okay. So we were together two years, and it didn't work out. One thing has nothing to do with the other, and you know it. When I met my wife, I hadn't seen or heard from you in years. What will it take to get that through your thick skull, woman?"

"Okay, but what about our child? How could you turn your back on your own kid?"

"Kid? What kid?" His eyes glittered with anger. "B..." he caught himself before he called her out of her name. "You're crazy. You were crazy back then and you're still crazy. Thank God I *didn't* have a kid with you."

"Don't you call me crazy," Margaret screamed. "Don't you ever call me crazy, Chauncey Graham," she screamed even louder. "You know we have a child. You walked out on me knowing full well I was pregnant." Margaret ranted uncontrollably. "Then you turned around and welcomed that witch of a woman into Holy Rock. You had to play the Good Samaritan, pretending like you were trying to help her get back on her feet after her husband died."

Pastor looked at her with marked curiosity. "How do you know all of this? You don't know anything about me or my wife, God rest her sweet soul."

"Sweet soul? You've got to be kidding me. You fell for that woman's Jezebel ways. Now you want to sit here and try to blame me for our breakup, all because of a little misunderstanding. Well, I'm not going to let that happen. I've been quiet for far too long. You may not have seen me, but you best believe I kept up with you—and her. When that witch died, I was so glad that I could have tap danced on her grave."

"You really are delusional. Seriously, you need help, Margaret. None of what you said happened, at least not the way you say it did." Pastor started the car.

Margaret jerked his hand off the ignition switch. "You knew that I was pregnant but you left me anyway."

Pastor pushed her hand away, turned off the ignition again and argued back. "First of all, when we broke up, I admit, you did tell me you were pregnant, but you also turned around and told me you lost the baby, that you had a miscarriage. Just like you lied to the cops about me raping you. And there was another time you told me you were pregnant but you said I was not the father. Another time you said you were pregnant then you turned around and said you weren't. You were always full of tricks."

"Okay, so I lied." Margaret began to cry.

"You're always lying. That's the problem." Pastor looked on, not sure what to say next. He could never be sure when she was telling the truth.

"We do have a kid! Do you hear me? We have a son!"

"And do you hear me? You're lying! I don't believe a word that comes out of your mouth. There is no kid." Pastor shook his head in total shock and dismay. This woman was definitely a whacko job. "What is it you want, Margaret? You're in Memphis for more than the church's Jubilee. You haven't returned in all of these years, so what makes this year so special? Why did you show back up here now? To try to send me to my grave? And what sick game are you playing with poor Pastor McCoy and his family? And don't tell me again about some kid cause you and I both know that's impossible. I would have known if I had a kid."

"I only told you that I had a miscarriage because you said things were over between us. But I didn't have a miscarriage. I was three months pregnant when I caught the bus and went back to Chicago. That's where I met Tonya. She was on her way back to Chicago too."

"Who is Tonya?"

"I just told you, the woman on the bus. Anyway, we became friends. I didn't have anyone I could talk to, and she was easy to talk to. My father wouldn't have had anything to do with me if he found out I was pregnant," she cried.

"Margaret," Pastor began calming down and becoming more sympathetic. "You're mixed up. A lot of what you think happened is in your mind."

"It's *not* in my mind. Stop telling me what's in my mind. Stop telling me that I'm crazy. You think I'm crazy because when I had our son I...I...tried to...to," she stuttered.

"Tried to what?"

"I tried to kill 'em. But I didn't, Chauncey. I didn't kill him. I only hurt him a little bit. I wasn't well back then, and Tonya, she got me some help so it was only right that I give her our baby."

Pastor sat in the driver's seat frozen like a block of ice as he listened to Margaret's tale.

"I gave her our baby so he would be safe. And he *was* safe. Even if it meant he had to grow up in Cabrini Green, he was still safe with her. I knew she would treat him good, real good and, and she had a husband and...and...and they promised that they would do right by him. I signed my parental rights over to her and her husband. That was a good thing too. I know it was. And when I got out of that God awful place, I went to see him and he was good so Tonya told me I should just let him stay. So I did. And she let me come see him from time to time as long as I didn't tell him that I was his mama. Wasn't that a good thing, Chauncey? God told me that I did good. And she had an older son so he had someone to play with." Margaret smiled, acting seemingly excited over what she'd said and done.

Shelia E. Bell

"If I believed a word of what you said, which I don't, you're telling me that you gave your kid to some woman you happened to meet on a bus?"

"Correction, I gave *our* kid, and she wasn't just some woman on a bus; she was my friend! But it was okay, Chauncey, because you see, later on I met someone else, and we fell in love. He didn't do me like you did me, and I forgot all about you. God gave me a second chance. Someone loved me again and I got pregnant." Margaret held her head between her hands and shook it from side to side.

Pastor realized that he was sitting across from someone who was clearly unstable. How much of what she was saying was true? And if it was true about her being pregnant by him all those years ago, he could possibly have a kid out there somewhere.

Margaret's eyes were glazed over. Her speech rapid as she kept talking. "I hate her. I hate her. I hate her. She took everything from me. I'm glad she's dead. I'm so glad she's dead, dead, dead. Ding dong, the wicked witch is dead."

"Who are you talking about? Who took everything from you?" Chauncey pushed.

"She came to visit me in Chicago. She was so nice. She bought me a blue dress. You know blue is my favorite color. She told me I should come stay with her and her husband for a while and she would take care of me until I got better. All I had to do was put her over my disability check and she would make sure I had everything I needed.

"So I did what she said. Her husband wasn't like you, Chauncey; he was a good man, but she didn't appreciate him. She was always so selfish. All he wanted was one thing, but noooo, she wouldn't give him what he wanted. She wouldn't give him a kid, so I gave him one. Simple as that. Of course, she was furious when she found out me and him had been sleeping together, but I didn't care 'cause I was in love. Plus, she always got what she wanted so it was my turn to be happy. He told me he was going to ask her for a divorce, and me, him and our baby would live happily ever after. But then he had a horrible accident, and, and he died." Margaret burst into another round of sobs.

"Margaret, let me get you back to the church so you can go home and get some rest. You're confused," Pastor said, this time his voice was full of empathy and pity. Margaret was clearly insane, yet oddly, part of him began to entertain some of what she said. He couldn't take any more. *I could have a kid? God, help us all if what she's saying is true.*

Margaret paid no mind to Hezekiah. "You think that wench just so happened to walk into Holy Rock all those years ago by chance? Humph, if you believe that then you're just as mixed up as you say I am."

"What are you saying, Margaret?"

"I'm saying that Audrey, the wicked witch, stole my baby! She always took everything from me," Margaret cried. "She hated me because her husband loved me and not her, but she never loved him. I loved him and he loved me." Margaret was distraught and kept on talking. "That's why she broke us apart," she rambled in and out of making sense to talking nonsense. "After her husband died, the man I loved, she stole my baby, Chauncey. Then the wicked witch sent me back to Chicago to that hospital and she made me give up my boy forever. I don't know how she did it, but everybody thought it was her kid. How could she do that? How could she make me give her my son? Why did she do that Chauncey? Why did she take my boy away from me? I already lost one son and she had to take my precious little baby. Now I don't have anything; both of my boys are gone."

Pastor felt his chest tighten and he laid his right hand over it.

"No need to try to have a heart attack on me. I heard you've had a few of 'em already, and I don't want no parts of it."

"How do you know Audrey?" Pastor's voice rose in anger.

"How do I know her? Haven't you heard a word I've said. She's my evil sister. I hated her then and I still hate her even if she is burning in hell. Me and her were never close as sisters, and thank God we didn't grow up together. Audrey was just like her mother. Daddy left my mother for Audrey's mother. Do you know that he married that woman three months after my mother divorced him?"

"Audrey, my Audrey? Your sister?"

"Yes, the wicked witch is my sister."

"This can't be true. Audrey never mentioned having a sister. And neither did you."

"Why would I tell you anything about her? She was a wicked witch."

"But Audrey had only one child when she and I met...Stiles."

"Only he wasn't her baby, he's mine!"

"You're saying that Stiles is your son?"

"That's exactly what I'm saying."

"Oh, my God," Pastor said, reeling from what Margaret had just told him.

"This can't be true. It's another one of your elaborate lies," a shaken Pastor said.

"Oh, it's true all right, and it's also true that you and me have a son. You just don't want to believe it because you're afraid I'll ask you for child support." She threw her head back in explosive laughter.

"Child support? Lord, have mercy. What is wrong with you?"

Margaret stopped laughing and started talking again as if Pastor had said nothing. "Our son is forty-one years old, so coming back to Memphis is like an anniversary to me. It's time to bring everything out in the open. I'm not getting any younger. I don't want to die with secrets untold. I need to tell both of them the truth."

"Lord, God, help us," Pastor cried out, trying to control his breathing and regain his composure.

"She stole my baby! Now it's time for me to stop hiding like I've been the one that was wrong. I want my sons to know the truth. I know it's going to be hard on them. They may even hate me. They may not want anything to do with me. But I have to do it. It's not fair to them."

"Both of your sons? If everything you're saying is true, then tell me where my kid is. Is he still in Chicago?"

"No, he's here."

"Here? Here as in Memphis?"

"Yes, here as in Memphis, you silly rabbit." Margaret laughed again and patted Pastor on his shoulder.

"He came here with you?" Pastor asked, visibly shaken and trying to process everything Margaret told him.

"Noooo, stop acting like a goofball, Chauncey. He didn't come with me. He lives here."

"He lives in Memphis? Where in Memphis does he live, Margaret?"

"In one of those suburbs. I forget the name of it. Anyway, you'll get a chance to meet him tomorrow."

"How is that?"

Shelia E. Bell

"Because he's the Senior Pastor of Holy Rock.

Pastor felt like he'd been stabbed in the heart. He couldn't breathe. He couldn't think straight. It took several seconds before he could speak. "That would mean that Pastor McCoy...is...woman, have you lost your freaking mind?" Pastor stopped talking.

"Not by a long shot. Only his birth name is Horace. Horace McKellar. I didn't know he was using an alias until a couple of years ago."

"Pastor McCoy...my son? I don't believe you. You need help, Margaret."

"You don't have to believe me. That won't change the truth. Anyway, as I was saying. My poor child and that sweet little wife of his got into a bit of trouble some years back."

"Trouble? What kind of trouble?"

"Embezzlement. They served time in prison; six whole years."

Pastor rubbed his head from front to back, shaking his head. "My God," he called out.

"Don't pretend like you're Mr. Perfect. Anyway, when they got released, they wanted a new start. Horace was called to the ministry and their lives just took off from there."

"I don't know what kind of game you're playing, but you're going to be sorry that you came to me with all of this craziness."

Once more, Margaret talked as if Pastor hadn't said a word. "After he got out of prison, I lost contact with him and Fancy. I didn't know what happened to my baby until I ran into Tonya's son one day at the Walmart. He told me that my boy moved to Memphis and was preaching at none other than, you guessed it, Holy Rock. It's true what folks say; it's a small world. Anywho, to make this loooong story short," she said, giggling, "I found my son.

I was a little confused to find out that he was no longer going by his birth name. When I contacted him, he swore me to secrecy, but he told me that the whole family had assumed new identities. And I know what you're going to ask me next. How did they do that if they're convicted felons? All I have to say is I don't know how they managed to do it, and frankly, I don't care. I'm just glad I found my boy again and wouldn't you know it, that lead me right back to my Stiles, too. I can't wait to tell them who I am. Thank you, Lord," Margaret said, raising her hands up, shaking her head. "Thank ya!"

Pastor couldn't move, couldn't speak. His whole body tightened. With every word Margaret spoke, his jaw became firmer, his muscles tightened, his heart more eager.

"My Horace, oops, I have got to stop calling him that. I wouldn't want to get him in a mess of trouble, you know. Anyway, as I was saying, Chauncey. Our son is a good child. Always has been. He's just like anybody else. He made some mistakes. But, so have I. You see, after you walked out on us, I had to do what I had to do. And Stiles, my poor baby. I had to stay away or the wicked witch would have sent me back to that terrible place. She would have had me locked up. You know she knows people. Being a witch, she had the power to send me away for good. But she's gone and I'm back. I just had to wait until the time was right."

"Lord, this can't be happening, and this can't be true," Pastor said in a troubling voice.

"I'm so glad that I didn't do like you did and walk out our child. I was there for Hezekiah after Tonya died, and I'm still here for him. Now I can be here for both of my children, even if it won't be for very long. You see, I'm not in the best of health. Got the same kinda cancer Tonya died from. Can you believe that, Chauncey?"

Chauncey barely shook his head. He was in shock.

"I don't know when the good Lord will call me home, so I want to do right by my boys. I want to tell them the truth. Don't you think it's ironic that both of my boys ended up being pastors, just like you, and that out of all the churches in this country, in this city, they ended up in Memphis...at Holy Rock. Our son is the senior pastor of the church you founded. Hah, how weird is that? And Stiles was the senior pastor before Hezekiah. Hah, God certainly does have a sense of humor." Her thin, silky eyebrows rose a trifle, and she let out a long exhalation of relief.

"Let me ask you something, Chauncey. How could you take my Stiles and raise him as your own and leave poor Hezekiah, your blood, out in the cold? How could you do that to me all over again? You're not a very nice person, Pastor Chauncey Graham. Not a very nice person at all."

With a horrified expression of disapproval, Pastor finally spoke. "I...I...I don't know what to say, except if Hezekiah is my son, how could you lie to my boy all of these years? How could you give him away to another woman, another man? You kept my son from me, denied me the opportunity to take care of him, to get to know him. If what you're saying is true, he wouldn't have gone through any of this mess you're talking about if you had just let me have him. And Stiles, poor Stiles. How is this going to affect him? They didn't get the chance to grow up together, to know each other as brothers. You robbed them. You want to blame this on me and Audrey, but you're the blame!" Disbelief, rage, and frustration were evident in the tone of his voice. "You're still the same lying, selfish, vindictive, revengeful woman you were back then. And you want to sit here and act like you're the victim."

"You can say what you want about me. For once, I don't care. This is not about you, Chauncey. For once, it...is...not...about...you. This time tomorrow, my sons will know everything. Yes, everything will be just perfect. Now, please, take me back to the church. I'm hungry again."

‡

Returning home that evening after the explosive meeting with Margaret, Pastor couldn't tell Josie what Margaret shared. He needed time to digest everything for himself, to analyze it and determine if all of what she said could be true. He told Josie he was going to do some last minute studying in preparation for his presentation at church the following day. She understood, and Pastor retreated to his home office to ponder over everything that Margaret had revealed.

He mindlessly paced across the hardwood floors in a devouring gulf of despair. *My son is Hezekiah McCoy? Audrey is Margaret's sister? Stiles is Margaret's son?*

Could everything she told him be true? And Audrey, what kind of woman had he been married to for all those years? If Audrey really did take Stiles as her own, then she was just as crazy as Margaret. This was like a daytime soap opera at its finest and Chauncey had a lot to think about. How would this revelation affect Stiles and Francesca? More importantly, how would it affect Hezekiah and Holy Rock? Pastor was beside himself with worry. He rested his head in his hands, closed his eyes, and prayed to God for direction, guidance, and forgiveness.

13

*I know they say there are a lot of fish in the sea, but
you're my Nemo.* Unknown

Khalil was impressed. From the outside alone, the
house looked twice as big as his parents' house. He
walked up to the door, rang the doorbell, and waited. It
didn't take long before the door opened and he was
greeted by a woman who introduced herself as Priscilla.
She ushered him inside, through the foyer, and into a
space he assumed was the family room.

Priscilla offered him a seat and asked him if she could
get something for him like water, soda, tea or something
stronger. He declined.

After sitting alone in the welcoming family room for
about five minutes, Dee appeared. She looked stunning,
even better than when he first met her. Khalil swallowed
hard.

"Hi, I'm sorry. I hope I didn't keep you waiting too
long," she said as she walked into the family room. For
the first time, Khalil noticed that something was wrong
with her right arm and hand. It dangled closely to her
body. It wasn't that he was annoyed or turned off by it, it
was just his observation.

He walked up to her and kissed her on the cheek.
"You're worth waiting for," Khalil said and smiled.

Dee smiled in return.

"This is a nice layout you got here," Khalil
complimented as he allowed his eyes to roam the
circumference of the spacious room.

"Thanks," she said as she led him to the wraparound
sofa and they sat down. "Can I get you something to
drink or eat?" she asked.

"No, uh, Priscilla already offered. Is she your mom?"

Dee laughed. "No, she's my live-in personal assistant."

"Dang, must be nice," Khalil said. "What line of work are you in?"

"I do some consulting and interior design on occasion. I used to be a nutritionist, but that was in another life." She laughed.

"Cool. Well, look you know, I told you I can't hang long this evening. I've already had a long day and I still have another obligation early tomorrow that was already in place this weekend. But I didn't want to miss the opportunity to spend a little time with you, find out where you live, and get to know you a little better."

"That's nice of you. So, what do you do for a living?" Dee asked.

"I work in the church."

"In the church? Please don't tell me you're a preacher," Dee said and laughed. "Although it would explain this early obligation you have tomorrow."

"Would that be so terrible?"

"Uhhh, no, not really. I guess it might help me earn a few brownie points with the man upstairs," Dee said and pointed upward toward the tall ceiling. "I sure could use a little divine favor right about now."

"Well, let me ease your pretty little mind. I am not a preacher. I'm a youth director."

"Youth director, huh? Interesting."

"Yeah, it can be quite interesting. And having my father as senior pastor adds a whole other dimension to it, you know."

"Soooo, a preacher's kid. Umm, this might be fun," Dee said.

"How is that?"

"Ohhh, nothing. But just so you know, I'm not into the church scene. I've had my share of going to church Sunday after Sunday or Wednesday night after Wednesday night for Bible study and mid-week praise. Uggh. I mean, enough already," Dee griped.

"Sounds like you and God have some beef."

"Not really. It's just that I've been there done that. I don't have anything against anyone for their beliefs or practices. I'm just talking about myself."

Khalil noticed again that she didn't use her right arm. It was just lying against her body.

"I heard that. Hey, if you don't mind me asking…"

Before he could complete his sentence, Dee spoke up. "I was in a car accident and lost the use of it," she snapped, casting her eyes downward.

Khalil pushed back. "Whoa, sorry. I just noticed that you weren't using it at all. I didn't mean to offend you."

"No, I'm the one who should say, sorry. I just get so tired of all the questions and stares from people, and I was wondering when you were going to mention it."

"Well, you answered me and I'm good with that. So, on to the next question."

Dee looked agitated again. "What is it?"

"What do you say about me and you going out to grab a bite to eat."

Dee relaxed, exhaled and smiled. "But you said you couldn't stay long."

"And I can't, but a man's got to eat doesn't he? And I've only had the equivalent of bird's food today."

"That sounds good, or if you like, I can ask Priscilla to prepare us something or go get us some take out."

"I don't want to put you or her through all of that. I'd rather the two of us just go grab something. We'll save the in house meal for a more suitable occasion," Khalil said.

76

"Okay, let's do it," Dee replied.

Khalil stood, extended his hand out toward hers, and helped her to her feet.

"Let me go get my purse, and I'll be ready," she told him. *This might work. This might work after all,* Dee thought as she dashed out the room.

‡

Khalil and Dee dined at a popular east Memphis Mexican restaurant. They communicated easily. He made her laugh and she made him want to get to know her better – much better. While dining, the age discussion came up. Khalil learned that Dee was sixteen years his senior, but they both made it clear that age was not a factor.

Dee confessed that she had been married before, and had a son, which again didn't bother Khalil one way or the other. She liked the fact that he seemed to be such an easygoing guy, but with a mature roughness around the edges that turned her on.

"You never said the name of the church you work at. Is it the same church where your father is the pastor?"

"Yes, my father is my boss. But it's all good. He allows me to have free reign when it comes to implementing youth programs and activities. I want the young people who participate in our youth programs to look at Holy Rock as a haven. Somewhere they can come and hang out, get involved in sports, arts, stay away from gangs, learn technology all in one place. Know what I mean?"

"Hold up. Did you say Holy Rock? Are you talking about the Holy Rock where Stiles Graham was the senior pastor? That Holy Rock?"

"Yep, you got it. Have you been there before?" Khalil asked.

"Uh, yes. I used to, well I used to belong there."

"Ummm, is that right?" Khalil looked intrigued. "You're no longer a member?"

"I don't think so. I'm sure my name was scratched off the church role a long time ago." She laughed. "You want to hear something funny?"

Khalil nodded. "Sure."

"I was the first lady of Holy Rock."

He swiped his forehead and cleared his throat. "Come again?"

"I was the first lady of Holy Rock," she repeated.

"You're joking right?"

"No, I'm not joking. It's the truth."

"You." He pointed at her. "You were the first lady? Ohhkay, but...how...who were you married to?" Khalil stammered.

"Stiles Graham. Small world, isn't it."

"Pastor Graham is your husband?"

"Correction. Ex-husband," Dee clarified.

Khalil shrugged, picked up his glass of water, and took a big gulp. "Oh well, guess his loss is my gain." He laughed and then without warning, he leaned over and kissed Dee on her lips.

‡

As if on special cue, Stiles entered the restaurant. The food at the banquet was superb, but it only kept the hunger panes at bay for a short time. His plan was to go to Pastor's house and hang out for a while, but he changed his mind after Pastor complained about being exhausted and still having to go over his speech for tomorrow's service. He enjoyed good Mexican food and he googled and found this restaurant was close to his hotel. He planned to order his food to go, then go to his hotel room, eat, and crash.

He perused the menu for a short while then made his order. He sat down at one of the booths and began toying with his phone. He texted Kareena to see how things were going with her and to tell her about the banquet, and his conversation with ex-wife number one.

A mariachi band appeared and began to entertain the crowd with song and dance moves. Stiles looked up from his phone. He couldn't believe who he saw sitting at a booth on the other side of the restaurant. It was Detria. At first a knot formed in his throat as he felt mounting anger and resentment. He quickly began to talk to himself. He had asked God to forgive him for his former actions, had asked Rena to forgive him, too, and promised that he would try to be a better person. The only way he felt that would happen was if he let go of the things that lay behind and move forward to the things in front of him.

Detria was laughing and talking to a guy who Stiles just assumed was her boyfriend. For a split second, hearing her laugh reminded him of the Detria he fell in love with.

The guy at the table stood up, said something to her, and then proceeded to walk in Stiles' direction. As the man walked past his booth, Stiles recognized him. It was one of Hezekiah's sons. At least that's who he strikingly resembled. Stiles hadn't gotten the chance to officially meet Hezekiah's boys, although this was no boy. Stiles got up and walked over to the booth where Detria sat.

Detria quickly looked up. "The devil himself," she said with a look of astonishment.

"I could say the same," Stiles responded drily.

She wondered what brought him to town. Maybe he had moved back; she didn't know. Her heart beat faster and she wanted to get up and pound him on his chest over and over again. She hated him for hating her.

"Hey, what's going on?" Khalil asked as he returned to the booth. Stiles stepped back, allowing the young man to slide back in the booth and sit down across from Detria.

"Aren't you Pastor McCoy's son?" Stiles asked.

"Yes, I am. I'm Khalil. His oldest. And you are?"

Stiles smiled while Detria flinched nervously. "Stiles Graham. Pastor Chauncey Graham is my father."

"Oh, yeah. We didn't have a chance to meet earlier at the banquet." Khalil extended his hand and the two men shook hands. "You were the pastor before my dad. I wasn't in Memphis then."

"Yeah, that's right. And no, we didn't get a chance to meet. I meant to stop and chat with your father, but I thought I'd give him a break and wait until tomorrow. You guys were surrounded by a crowd of well-wishers."

"You got that right. I never shook so many hands, and hugged so many little old ladies. I felt like a politician for a minute." Khalil chuckled then looked at Dee and then back at Stiles. He gestured between the two of them. "So you're her ex?"

"Right," Dee responded before Stiles. "Khalil, honey, do you mind if we get our food to go. I've lost my appetite."

Khalil paused before responding. "Uh, yeah, sure."

"Don't leave on my account. I didn't mean to interrupt your meal. I called in a to-go order and I saw you sitting over here. Just thought I'd come over and say hello. I didn't think it would be right to see you and not speak. So, hello, Detria."

"Goodbye, Stiles," Detria said vehemently.

"Excuse me," the server said and refilled their drinks.

"Could we get a couple of carry out containers?" Khalil took the opportunity to ask the server.

"Of course. I'll be right back."

"Well, it was good to meet you, Khalil. I'm looking forward to tomorrow. I know Holy Rock is going to be on fire," Stiles said as he began to walk off. He stopped and looked over his shoulder. "Will you be there tomorrow, Detria?"

Detria didn't respond. Her eyes blazed with contempt as she watched him walk away.

The server returned with carryout containers, and the couple left the restaurant. On the drive, Dee was unusually quiet. Khalil didn't know what to make of the personality change. It had to be because she saw her ex back at the restaurant. He wondered how their relationship ended. Was he one of those dudes like his dad, who was known to have an occasional wandering eye? Khalil didn't address it with his dad, but was well aware that his father flirted with some of the women at Holy Rock because he'd observed him firsthand.

"Hey, what's up with the silent treatment? Dude must have really broken your heart 'cause now you're breaking mine by not talking," Khalil said as he turned into Dee's driveway and parked.

Detria looked at Khalil and gave him a smile. "It's not like that. It's just that I haven't seen my ex since our divorce. I didn't know how I would react seeing him again, but now I know."

"So what is it that you know?"

"That I still despise him," Dee said. "But it is what it is. Would you like to come inside, have a glass of wine?"

"I really need to go. I told you I have a long day tomorrow. It's our Jubilee. Hey, why don't you come?"

Dee looked at him awkwardly, tilted her head slightly, and grinned. "You're kidding me, right?"

"No, I'm serious. I'd love to have you there." Khalil said, then hopped out of his car and walked to the passenger side to open the door for her.

"Thank you," Dee said, and proceeded to get out of the car. "Come in, let's have that glass of wine and we'll talk about it."

"Okay, sure."

Once inside, Dee stepped out of her shoes, took hold of Khalil's hand, and led him into the chef style kitchen. She went to the built in wine cooler. "You choose," she said, opening the door to a display an array of expensive white and red wines.

"I'm not good at this. During my teen years, I was more of an herb connoisseur," he said and laughed. "If you know what I mean."

"Yes, I definitely know what you mean." Dee laughed too. "If that's your indulgence, then it's nothing but a word."

Khalil waved her off. "No, no, no. That was then. I don't mess around with anything other than a little social drinking every now and then."

"I'm just saying, if you change your mind, then let me know. I definitely can accommodate you. Will you get that one?' she pointed to a particular bottle of red wine.

"Sure." Khalil removed a bottle of red wine out of its slot, and Dee retrieved two wine glasses out of the cabinet, expertly using her one good hand. "The opener is in that drawer right about the cooler," she told him.

"Gotcha. To new friendships," Khalil said after he opened the wine and poured each of them a glass.

They clicked their glasses together and then each took a sip before setting the glasses on the island.

"Whaddaya say we go relax a little."

"Cool," he replied.

"Follow me," Dee said.

Khalil picked up their wine glasses and Dee led him down a long hallway and into her master suite that resembled a mini apartment.

She sat down on the sofa, patted her hand on the space next to it, and Khalil sat down next to her. He passed her her glass of wine and they each took a few sips before sitting their glasses down on the table next to the sofa.

Khalil reached in, took Dee around her waist, and pulled her into him. His lips devoured hers with long, passionate kisses while his hands familiarized themselves with her body. Khalil kept kissing her and then pulled back only long enough to stand, pick her up, and carry her to the king sized bed.

Dee didn't protest; she welcomed his warm kisses. The touch of his hands set her body on fire. She didn't care how much younger he was or how much older she was, all she wanted was to be loved and needed, and for now Khalil was giving her exactly what she wanted.

14

Conscience is what hurts when everything else feels so good. Unknown

Pastor was able to get a couple hours of sleep at the most. After seeing Margaret, and learning all that he had, he didn't think he would be able to go to church or if he even wanted to go. He didn't know if Margaret had told Hezekiah and Fancy what she'd told him, so he didn't know what he should expect when he walked through the doors of Holy Rock. He didn't know what to tell Stiles, if anything, and he still hadn't mentioned anything to Josie.

He didn't have much time to worry about it because the doorbell rang. Was it Hezekiah? Had Margaret told him that he was his father? He walked out of the bedroom, where he was getting dressed, and up the hall.

"I'll get it," Pastor called out to Josie who was in the kitchen making coffee and breakfast. Pastor was elated when he answered the door and saw Francesca and Tim. He had no idea they had decided to come to Memphis for today's celebration. With all the mess Margaret promised to bring up to the family later that evening, Pastor reveled in this temporary moment of peace. He looked at his daughter and overwhelming joy filled his heart. God had been good and gracious because Francesca couldn't look any more healthier. The face mask she wore was the only thing that reminded him of her illness.

Stiles came over to the house shortly after Francesca and Tim arrived. Again, Pastor was reminded of all the things Margaret had revealed. *Stiles is Margaret's son. God, how will he accept it when she tells him?*

He managed to push the thoughts out of his mind, albeit temporary. It felt like old times for him with

Stiles and Francesca together at the house they grew up in. If only Audrey was here to witness this, but Josie replaced his loving wife, and Margaret was about to cause an explosion that Pastor felt could tear his family apart forever.

How would Stiles and Francesca come to terms with it all? How would they accept Hezekiah as their brother? Pastor didn't know if he was prepared for the days' events to unfold. He tried to hide his fear and prayed to God for everything to work out. Margaret could act irrationally at times, which is why he wasn't all too surprised when she told him she had been institutionalized more than once back in the day. The way things were about to go down, and with Margaret making a surprise trip to Memphis, he didn't know what else the crazy woman might have on her mind. Maybe all of this was a game, a ploy to get him worked up for nothing. Surely, Margaret wouldn't want to hurt her relationship with Hezekiah because that was exactly what she would be doing if she told him that she was his birth mother. Hezekiah was forty-one years old and now she wanted to open Pandora's box. And Stiles, well things would be just as hard on him, too.

Pastor prayed for a miracle, that God would hold that woman's tongue. He tried to push away thoughts about what might happen and enjoy the time with his kids before it was time to leave for church.

Josie served breakfast and the five of them laughed and talked. Pastor took in the faces of his kids and his wife. Inwardly, he thanked God for this reunion. Something in his spirit told him to enjoy this time and not worry. He thought about the Bible verse, *Do not worry about tomorrow… Today has enough trouble of its own.*

‡

Hezekiah called the ministers into a brief meeting to go over the day's schedule. He didn't behave any differently so Pastor believed that Margaret had kept her mouth shut.

"Pastor," Hezekiah said as they walked side by side into the sanctuary.

"Yes, Pastor McCoy," Pastor replied, trying his hardest to act as normal as possible. This was not the time or place to talk to Hezekiah about the things Margaret had said.

"I'd like to invite you, Sister Josie, and Reverend Graham for an early supper at my house. My Aunt Margaret stayed up half the night cooking, and we would love for you to join us in celebrating Jubilee."

Pastor didn't know what to say. He was skeptical because he didn't know if this had been Margaret's idea or not. Maybe she planned to tell her ridiculous story over dinner. He didn't know.

"Uh, Sister Josie already prepared our Sunday meal, and well I have to see if Stiles has plans." Pastor said, trying to make an excuse. "Oh, and my daughter and her husband surprised me this morning. They drove from Newbern, Tennessee to be here today."

"Bring them too and tell Sister Josie to put that food up until tomorrow. How would it look if I'm celebrating this day without the man who is responsible for the existence of Holy Rock? That wouldn't be right now, would it?"

"I guess when you put it like that," Pastor replied sullenly. "Okay, Josie and I will be there. I'll check with Stiles and my daughter to see if they'll be able to come along, too."

Hezekiah patted Pastor on his back. "Good. Now let's go praise the Lord."

The ministerial staff, which included Pastor, walked into the sanctuary followed by Hezekiah. After several songs by the choir and guest choirs, Pastor was introduced and he walked up nervously to the podium.

"To God be the Glory," Pastor said as he stood at the podium. "For the great things He has done. I feel mighty blessed today. I thank God that I'm alive, breathing, and in reasonable health and strength. I thank him that I'm able to celebrate this day. It means a lot to me. I want to thank Pastor McCoy," Pastor said, and looked over his shoulder at Hezekiah who was sitting in his usual spot in the pulpit, "for allowing me this time to share with you, Holy Rock, how grateful to God I am for the vision he gave me to preach His Word." He hoped his uneasiness didn't show. He said a prayer in his spirit and kept on talking.

He looked out on the congregation and saw Josie, Stiles, Francesca, and Tim sitting together on the third row behind Fancy and her entourage. He still didn't see Margaret, so he pushed everything else out of his mind and concentrated on the task ahead. He smiled when he also saw Rena and her parents. He wondered if Stiles had seen Rena at the banquet last night. If so, he hadn't mentioned it.

"I was a much younger man than I am now when God called me to preach his word at a little church right here in Memphis. It was old, run down and had a total of twenty-five people on the church roll, and fifteen of the twenty-five members were related to each other." Pastor chuckled and so did many in the sanctuary. "The name of the church at the time was Rock of Ages. The pastor was Reverend Glen James. He was eighty years old when he took me under his wing. He taught me a lot. Reverend James never attended theology school, didn't have a divinity degree. He didn't even have a high school diploma and could barely read. But one thing he knew that no one could take away from him was the Word of God. He carried the Word around with him in his heart. Under his tutelage, I came to know and see Christ in a whole new light."

Pastor continued talking and the people listened intently. Stiles was impressed and proud with Pastor and what he shared. He had heard the story only once before, but today it was if he was hearing it for the very first time.

"I stayed at Rock of Ages until God called Reverend Glen home to glory. The small membership decided that they would disband and go join other churches. God spoke to me through one of the members. He told me to pray and seek God about starting my own church. I followed his godly counsel and Holy Rock was born."

The congregation including First Lady Fancy, Stiles, Tim, Josie and Francesca stood up and applauded. "Amen" and "Praise the Lord" rang throughout the sanctuary.

As they took their seats, Francesca continued listening to Pastor talk about how much God had blessed him and his family. Being back at Holy Rock, and seeing her father in the pulpit, brought on memories of her growing up at the church. She thought about all the fun times she had running through the church, attending children's church, pulling childish pranks and as she got older attending youth night. Her thoughts turned to memories she didn't want to resurrect, but nevertheless they pushed their way through. The memory of Pastor Travis, the youth minister that molested her in his office. Her cousin, Fonda, who did the same thing. What made them think they could destroy her whole life the way they had. Everything changed for her when that happened. She didn't feel that she could tell anyone, especially knowing that her mother knew what Fonda did to her and she didn't do or say anything, except blame Francesca. It wasn't enough that Pastor Travis left Holy Rock or that later on he was charged with molesting other girls at another church. None of that helped because the damage had already been done to her and she would never be able to erase it.

Tim squeezed her hand, which pulled her from the painful thoughts racing through her mind. Francesca looped her arm through her husband's arm and focused on the service. After Pastor finished speaking, a guest soloist sang, followed by a praise dancer, and then Pastor McCoy came to the podium to deliver the Word.

Hezekiah looked out at the thousands of people packed into the sanctuary like sardines in a can. Extra chairs had been placed at the end of each pew, every one of them filled. The overflow rooms were filled to capacity. Chairs had to be placed in the vestibule, too. It was a blessed day.

Hezekiah envisioned the amount of money that was collected in all three offerings today. Yes, it was going to be a day of divine favor. He smiled from ear to ear then looked at his iPhone to read the text for today's message.

"What a mighty God we serve," Hezekiah started "This day symbolizes forty years that this house of God has been in place. It is certainly a time of Jubilee. You heard the man of God tell you that it hasn't always been easy. You heard him give you the history of this great temple of God. You heard him tell you how God has seen him through. Well, I'm here to tell you that God is a good God. He's seen me through and he's seeing you through.

Praises be to God. I want you to go with me to second Corinthians eighth chapter. I'll be reading from the Jubilee Bible translation. Listen to what the word of God says. Brothers and sisters, we want to let you know about the grace of God that was given to the churches of Macedonia. While they were being tested by many problems, their extra amount of happiness, and their extreme poverty resulted in a surplus of rich generosity. I assure you that they gave what they could afford and even more than they could afford, and they did it voluntarily.

"Holy Rock, just like the Corinthians, I need you to recommit to giving to God. I need you to give until you can't give any more. I'm telling you, God will bless you for it. He will take care of you. He's the God of more than enough. If you want to experience his goodness, then you must follow his ways. Give generously today and every Sunday. I challenge each of you to increase your giving beyond mere convenience and into the realm of sacrifice."

He walked to the level surface of the sanctuary, walking from one end to the other, preaching with boldness. Hezekiah preached for the next thirty minutes. When he opened the doors of the church, it looked like hundreds of people came forward. Yes, God was blessing him at Holy Rock and Hezekiah couldn't be happier.

When he saw his Aunt Margaret walking toward the altar from somewhere in the back of the sanctuary, forced tears streamed down his face. She approached one of the deacons and whispered something in his ear. In turn, the deacon walked over to the front of the altar where Hezekiah stood and whispered something in his ear.

Pastor almost choked when he saw her come forward. *God, what is she doing?*

"Holy Rock, I want to stop right here for a minute." Hezekiah raised up one hand. The congregation settled and the musicians halted. "I didn't tell you that my aunt traveled from Chicago just to be here to celebrate Jubilee with me and my family. I haven't seen her in quite some time, so I'm especially grateful for her sacrifice. God has touched her spirit and she wants to say a few words. Aunt Margaret, let us hear what you have to say."

Margaret stood close by Hezekiah. Pastor was next to the other ministers and deacons who were lined up next to Hezekiah to welcome those who had come up for prayer or to join the church. *What is she about to say? I know she didn't just get a revelation from the Lord. The devil maybe,* Pastor thought to himself.

Margaret rocked slowly from side to side, both arms folded inside each other like a tied ribbon.

"Praise God, hallelujah," she said. "I'm glad to be here today. I'm glad that I was able to come to Memphis to celebrate this special occasion. It means more than you can ever think or imagine. I need to get some things said today, cause I don't have much longer on this earth. You see, the doctors say I have a terminal illness and that I don't have long to live. But God is able."

Hezekiah and many of the other ministers and congregation were shocked by this bit of news. "The devil is a liar. By His stripes you are healed," Hezekiah proclaimed.

"Thank you, Pastor McCoy," Margaret answered.

Some people were still standing and others had taken their seats. People continued with their praises and amens as Margaret spoke.

"You know it is truly a blessing to have Pastor McCoy as your senior pastor, as your shepherd, the leader of the flock. He's a good man. He's a mighty good man," Margaret continued.

Hezekiah smiled, his chest poked out. He extended his hand out toward First Lady Fancy and she walked up to stand next to her husband while Margaret continued her praises. He placed his arm around his wife with pride.

"You couldn't have found better leaders than Pastor McCoy and former senior pastor, Stiles Graham."

Stiles nodded and mouthed the words, "Thank you, Jesus."

"Holy Rock, it hasn't always been like this. You see, God don't like ugly. Sometimes he'll let you think you're getting away but you can't hide from God. He'll bring your sins to the light."

Hezekiah's expression began to change slightly to an inquisitive stare. What was she talking about? He looked down at Fancy and lightly squeezed her shoulder. Fancy looked up at him in wonderment.

"Pastor McCoy is a good man, a God-fearing man. I thank God every day for him. Holy Rock, I won't rest until I let you know that this man is a warrior, a soldier for God." She turned and looked at Hezekiah. "But, baby, there's something I've been holding in for a mighty long time. I just can't keep quiet about it. It wouldn't be fair to you...or to Reverend Stiles."

Stiles looked confused. Pastor looked like he would pass out at any minute. Hezekiah looked at Margaret inquisitively, recognizing that his aunt was more than likely about to say something inappropriate. "It's okay, Aunt Margaret. We'll talk about it later," he said, walking up next to her and placing his arm around her shoulders. He wanted to soothe the woman and at the same time make her stop all the babbling. She was way out of line with whatever she was about to say. With his eyes, he signaled his armor bearers to come forward.

Margaret ignored his gesture and slightly pushed him away.

"Yes. Amen. All right now," people were saying.

"No, I have to say this now, Pastor McCoy. You see, I won't be going back home," she said looking at him with a crazed expression plastered on her otherwise attractive countenance. "There's something I have to let you know, baby, and Holy Rock, your pastor is going to need your support. I need you to be here for him."

You could hear the congregation mumbling. Some people looked at each other in confusion, then an eerie hush came over the church.

Hezekiah whispered in Margaret's ear to have a seat, but it was to no avail.

"Lord, God, not now. Not here," Pastor whispered to himself and the good Lord.

"I don't know how else to say this other than to say it. I am not your aunt, honey. All those years Tonya and her husband raised you because I couldn't. I wasn't in a good place back then. What I'm trying to say is Tonya, God rest her sweet soul, was not your mother. I'm your birth mother and that man right there, who you know as Pastor, is your father."

Hezekiah reeled from the words that poured from her lips. Fancy ran up next to him and grabbed him around the waist. Two armor bearers tried to lead Margaret away but she adamantly refused to budge.

"Holy Rock, I'm telling you what God loves–and that's the truth. Hezekiah, honey, I want you and everyone to know, about your daddy." Her voice escalated. "He left you fatherless so he could start a life with another woman. She was no stranger either; she was my sister. She not only broke up my family but she stole my other son from me, too. She was nothing but a wicked witch, Satan's pawn. Some of you long time Holy Rock members remember her. I'm talking about Audrey Graham. May she rest in hell. And, Hezekiah, baby, your daddy, I hate to say is a no good, lying, hypocrite." Margaret pointed to Pastor. "Just look at 'em, standing over there like he's so perfect when he's nothing but a liar and a cheat. Isn't that right, Chauncey Graham!"

The armor bearers surrounded her, trying to lead her away, but somehow as they wrestled with her as gently but forcibly as they could, she rocked and reeled as they tugged on her but she refused to be moved. "He's far from being a man of God! And Stiles, sweetheart, Audrey Graham, the witch he made his wife, was just as bad because you're my son, my baby boy. She took you away from me when you were a baby! But mama's here now, even if it's only for a short time. Mama's here for both of you."

The congregation exploded. Hezekiah and Fancy stood deftly still like they'd been transformed into cement. Pastor's shoulders slumped as his eyes locked in with Josie, Francesca and Stiles. Francesca turned what seemed two shades darker. Her hand flew up to her covered mouth. Her knees grew weak. She would have collapsed if Tim hadn't grabbed her around the waist to hold her up. A deep frown caressed Stiles' forehead as he tried to digest what Margaret had just said. Josie held on to the pew in front of her.

"You know what God loves. He loves the truth. And if you don't believe anything I have to say, please believe that your Mama loves you Hezekiah and Stiles." Margaret looked at Hezekiah, then Stiles and then out into the sea of people.

"Oh, my God," Fancy screamed in horror, placing her hand over her chest.

Khalil and Xavier ran up and stood beside their mother. Xavier grabbed her and Khalil wrapped his arm around his father's shoulder and tried to lead him away.

Without warning, and with quickness, Margaret jerked her right arm away from the armor bearer, quickly reached into her purse and whipped out a Glock 19 semiautomatic pistol. In shock and awe, instead of bum rushing her, the armor bearer impulsively jumped back as screams reverberated throughout the sanctuary. Before the deacons and armor bearers could take her all the way down, multiple shots rang out. Bullet after bullet sprayed through the congregation sounding louder than a church bell ringing on Sunday morning. Panicked and frightened, people took off running in every direction, some pushing, stumbling and stepping over each other. What a Jubilee celebration it was.

15

*Realize deeply that the present moment
is all you ever have.* Elkhart Tolle

Rena stood in front of the twenty-first floor window of her hotel suite and glared outside as thunderstorms raged, the lightning clapped, and hail pounded against the building. It sounded and looked like the world was coming to an end. It was mid-afternoon, but it was almost pitch black outside. Tornado sirens started blaring and Rena turned and stepped away from the window. "Robert, I need you. God, let him get here soon. Please, God," she continually pleaded as she folded her arms and went and laid down on the hotel bed.

She couldn't erase the memories of what she had experienced less than 24 hours ago. Seeing the blood soaked bodies of her parents laying inches in front of her was something she would forever remember. One minute she and her parents were listening to that crazy, evil woman and the next minute they were trying to duck behind the church pew to escape the barrage of bullets sailing through the sanctuary. It proved to be a hopeless situation for her mom and dad.

She looked at her clothes that were on the floor in a corner of the hotel room, the clothes that she had on that awful day, and burst into sobs when she saw all of the blood splatter on her dress, shoes, even her purse. She tried to block out the look on her mother's face. Her mother died with her eyes open and it looked like she was searching for something. Her father's eyes were closed and one arm lay across his chest while the other one was spread across her mother like he was trying to protect her.

Rena cried as she got up off the bed and looked at her parents' luggage and various items of clothing they had left sprawled around the room. She couldn't sleep, couldn't eat, couldn't do anything but weep. She needed Robert but his flight wouldn't be arriving until later that evening. It was like time had stood still and was moving at a snail's pace. So much had happened in so little time that she couldn't focus. The thought of Frankie being dead and her husband, Tim too? It was unfathomable. To think about all the years Frankie had put up such a long, brave fight against her AIDS/HIV, only to succumb to a bullet by some crazy maniacal woman that wanted to exact revenge on Pastor Graham and his dead, wicked wife, Audrey. Rena felt like she was in the middle of a horror movie. People were so full of rage and anger in the world today, and it was hard to comprehend. But to take the lives of her parents, who were always good people that cared about others, was appalling. And maybe Frankie had done her dirt in her time, but she had put all of that behind her and seemed to have a happy relationship with her husband. All of that had been snuffed out in a matter of seconds and Rena felt that the weight of her grief would drown her.

Inside she couldn't put out the fuel that was beginning to blaze in her heart. She thought about how her life had taken a turn for the very worst ever since the Graham family entered into it. It had been Francesca who introduced her to lesbianism. It was because of Francesca that she walked around to this day with an incurable STD. Audrey Graham despised her and did everything she could at every turn to make her life a living hell. Then there was Stiles, Mr. Self-Righteous Stiles Graham who made her feel like she was less than nothing, who divorced her and threw her aside like last night's garbage.

The whole family, except for Pastor Graham, had been nothing but cruel, evil, and mean towards her. But nothing could trump what had happened this time. This time her parents paid the ultimate price because of the Grahams. This time there would be no turning back, no way to make things better. Her parents were dead and they were dead because of the Grahams. She could never ever forgive them, or herself. She should never have gotten mixed up with them in the first place.

"Robert, please hurry," she cried out. She began to shake as the images played over and over in her mind. "Oh, God, God, I need you, God. I need you now," she continually prayed and wept aloud, rocking back and forth. "How can I find the strength to bury my parents? How will I make it through this?" The traumatizing ache over the people she'd lost felt like a boulder had fallen on her heart. Her FaceTime chimed. She opened it to her sister and brother on the phone. She rarely talked to them, not because she didn't love her siblings, but because they were so much older. Being a change of life baby, when she was born, they had long left home and moved out of state. Rena grew up feeling like an only child. But now they needed each other. Hopefully, together, maybe they would find some tiny bit of consolation in being family.

‡

Robert Becton stood outside the terminal of Memphis International Airport impatiently waiting on Uber to pick him up and take him to his wife. The heavy rainstorms and dark clouds welcomed him to the murderous city.

He was anxious to get to Rena. He knew she shouldn't have come to Memphis. She had traveled to Memphis several times since moving back to Andover, but there was something about this visit that troubled him. Granted, he didn't exactly explain it to Rena. Instead, she thought he was jealous about the possibility of her seeing Stiles again. That wasn't it at all, not really. Sure, he didn't like the hold that Stiles seemed to still have on Rena, but this time things were different. When she told him that she and her parents were going to Memphis, uneasiness settled over him that even he couldn't explain. Now he understood the reason he felt the way he had.

When he heard Rena's voice and saw on FaceTime the look of anguish on her face his heart seemed to break in a million tiny pieces. He couldn't fathom what she was going through in Memphis all alone. He only knew that he had to get to her as fast as he possibly could. He couldn't make sense out of what Rena told him; she was way too distraught to be coherent. From what he read online, the pastor's aunt had massacred people for no reason, not that any reason would ever justify what the woman had done.

Her rampage only came to an end after she was shot by one of the armor bearers. Another armor bearer knocked her down, and violently removed the gun from out of her hands. From what he'd read, the woman died later that night from her wounds.

The Uber driver pulled up and Robert hurriedly climbed inside the Toyota Camry. *I'm on my way, baby. Just hang on. I'm coming.*

16

Everyone loves justice in the affairs of another. Proverb

Detria had remained glued to either the television or her computer most of the day and well into the night, following the news about the shooting at Holy Rock. She was heartbroken over the devastation that woman had caused. However, she wasn't overly concerned about the accusations that Margaret revealed about Audrey not being Stiles' biological mother. In some small way she felt that Stiles deserved the sudden turnaround in his life, and Audrey definitely deserved to have her good, wholesome name tarnished.

When she got a call from Khalil the night following the shooting, she quickly invited him to come over, knowing that he could probably use a shoulder to lean on after all that had transpired. She felt somewhat flattered that Khalil would even think about calling her, let alone visiting her, during a tragic time as this. She was thankful that his family was not among the tragedies. According to Khalil, his little brother, who was wounded, had been treated and released from the hospital.

It was after eleven p.m. when the doorbell rang, way past Priscilla's bedtime. Rain was coming down hard, but Priscilla was a hard sleeper, so Detria knew that she probably wouldn't hear anything anyway, not that she cared. She hurried to the door, opened it, and met a slightly wet and distraught looking Khalil. He almost looked like a child, but from their previous visit, she knew beyond a shadow of a doubt that he was a full grown man...in every way. She dismissed the lustful thought, reached out and removed the umbrella from his hand, and ushered him into the house.

"Khalil, baby, I'm so sorry about what happened. How is your family?" she asked as they walked hand in hand and into the kitchen.

"Not good, Dee. I mean everybody's trying to make sense out of what happened. I don't understand any of it. I had to get out of there. That's why I came here. I know it's late, so I won't stay long."

"No, stay as long as you want. As a matter of fact, I think you should stay the night. You need to be away from it all, if only for a while." She stroked his back and offered him a seat at the massive kitchen peninsula. "Let me make you a good stiff drink."

Khalil didn't refuse. Being a former drug addict, he knew he shouldn't indulge in any mind altering substances like hard liquor, but tonight was different, considering all that he had witnessed. He agreed with Dee that he needed something to take the edge off.

"The glasses are over there in that cabinet to the right. If you'll get one and put some ice in yours if you'd like, that would be straight."

Khalil walked over to the cabinet, retrieved a glass, walked over to the stainless steel refrigerator and placed the glass underneath the ice dispenser until a couple of cubes fell into it. Without saying anything, he returned to the peninsula and sat in the high back stool.

"Here you go. Help yourself," she said, returning from her fully stocked bar with a bottle of brown liquor, placing it in front of him.

Khalil poured himself a stiff drink, brought the glass up to his lips, and the liquid disappeared without a trace. He shook his head and grimaced like he was in pain.

"Another one?" she asked.

This time Khalil responded by sliding the glass toward her and Dee complied by pouring him another shot.

"You can't imagine seeing what I witnessed yesterday, Dee," Khalil said, finishing off the second drink as quickly as he had the first. "I'm just glad my family is okay, well most of them anyway. Aunt Margaret is dead but the things she said, I'm totally puzzled about."

"If you want to talk about it, I'm here," Detria told him. "Another?" she offered a third time.

Khalil nodded his head. "Yeah, one more. I want to forget it all, everything that happened, but it keeps playing over and over again in my head." He grabbed the side of his head with both hands like he could somehow squeeze the memories out.

"Why don't you come lie down for a while? Try to get some sleep." Dee gently rubbed his back in a circular motion then stopped and gently tugged on his hand.

Khalil didn't protest. He gulped down the last drink, then stood up and allowed Dee to guide him to her bedroom. She turned back the covers on the bed when they entered the room and without prompting, he walked over to the bed, sat down, took off his shoes, and laid back. The liquor had relaxed him and he closed his eyes as his head rested on the soft fluffy pillow.

Dee was already dressed in her nightgown and robe. She removed her robe and went to the other side of the king bed, got in and pulled the covers over her legs, but she sat in the bed rather than lay down in it. Looking over at Khalil, she didn't say a word. She heard his light snore and proceeded to put some cover over him. Flooded suddenly with memories of her baby girl's death, she fought against crying but became overwhelmed thinking about the loss of so many people, but especially Francesca and her husband and Rena's parents.

She may not have seen eye to eye with Stiles, Pastor, or Rena, but she didn't wish the pain of losing a loved one on anyone. Eyeing Khalil, she leaned in next to him and kissed him on the side of his head. He didn't stir. Easing up out of the bed, she went into the bathroom, closed the door behind her, sat on the toilet, and allowed the tears to come. The pain in her heart that she felt for Khalil, for herself, and even for Stiles, was paramount. No amount of discord or dislike for Stiles or his father could make her feel any less sorry for what they must be going through. Francesca's death must be ripping them apart.

Her thoughts transferred to her own little boy, three year old Elijah. It wasn't often that she saw him or spent any significant time with him. He unofficially lived with his father, Skip, and Skip's wife, Meaghan. Detria initially fought against Elijah living with his daddy, but in the beginning when she was incapacitated from the car accident, she had to admit that she wasn't the best mother. Her physical challenges limited her ability to care for her son in the manner she desired.

As the boy spent more time with Skip, Elijah preferred being with him more than he did with her. Priscilla told her it was because Elijah had a younger sibling and enjoyed having someone to play with. Detria wasn't buying it. She believed that her little boy simply preferred his daddy over her. She soon came to terms with it and to keep her son happy she let him stay as long as he wanted to stay. He visited her a day or two every month and most holidays, but other than that, it was like Detria didn't have a kid.

Her cell phone rang. She got up off the toilet and went back into the bedroom, taking caution not to awaken Khalil. The phone continued to ring then stopped before she could follow the ring. Next, her house phone rang. She looked at Khalil, and he still hadn't budged. *He must really be exhausted,* she thought and proceeded to pick up the phone from its base.

"Uggh, the devil himself," she mumbled when she saw it was Skip calling. She pushed the button to answer. "Hello, why are you calling me this time of night?" she whispered as she went back into the bathroom and closed the door. "You must have dialed the wrong number; I am not your booty call."

"Thank God for small miracles," he shot back. "Look, Meaghan said that I should call and let you know that we had to take Elijah to the ER."

"So Meaghan had to tell you to call me? Uggh. Anyway, what happened? Is he okay?" she asked, a little panicked.

"Don't get your panties in a wad. He's fine. He did an awkward flip on the bed earlier this evening, landed on his arm, and broke his wrist. He's a real trooper. Didn't cry or anything."

"I hope my son is okay. You need to watch him more closely," she chastised Skip.

"Look, I didn't call for all the unnecessary drama. I told you that he's fine. I just wanted to keep you in the loop of what's going on with him."

"Is he asleep?" She figured that he was since it was after midnight.

"Yeah, he's knocked out."

"Call me in the morning so I can talk to him."

"Yeah," he answered drily and then ended the call.

Detria heard the phone go silent so she pushed the END button on her phone. She looked at herself in the mirror. Sometimes she didn't like the person that she had become. So much had happened in her life that she wasn't proud of. Physically abusing Pastor was one, lying about Stiles physically abusing her was another, cheating on him was yet another, not being the best mother she could be to her daughter, and now repeating the same with her son. Her list of mess-ups was endless. Even before then, she used to be manipulative and sneaky. As close as she was to her sister, even Brooke knew little of the stuff Detria had done.

When she first returned to Memphis, setting her eyes on Stiles was another one of her manipulative feats. It paid off for a while, at least, because she got Stiles to fall in love with her and marry her. His mother loved her probably because as Audrey told her, they were two of a kind. They saw what they wanted and refused to stop until they got whatever it was. Detria smiled a bit as she thought about Audrey, but soon her smile was replaced by tears as she started thinking about her failed marriage, the death of her baby girl, and the car accident that left her in constant pain.

After crying for several minutes, Detria washed her face and returned to bed. She nestled against Khalil who turned over toward her and embraced her tightly. Without saying a word, he kissed her on her forehead and his hands traveled the course of her curvaceous body. She reciprocated by kissing him on his lips and performing her own exploration while helping him out of his clothes. Both of them needed a way out, a reprieve from everything going on around them. Dee wanted the memories to stop tormenting her, memories that hadn't left her alone since Baby Audrey died. Today's events had taken her back to that awful place of pain and anguish—a place that Khalil would come to know all too well for himself.

Dee lay underneath Khalil. She felt protected, safe, and needed. It didn't matter about their age difference. It didn't matter anymore what other people thought about her. All that mattered was now, this moment in time. Khalil expertly made love to her while she listened to the mounting storm outside and the strong force of winds pounding against her windowpane. All was right in her world and she couldn't care less about anyone else.

17

Come back. Even as a shadow, even as a dream.
Euripides

Half past midnight.

Pastor, Josie, and Stiles approached the front door of Pastor's house, all in a state of disbelief. Pastor walked inside the house, shoulders drooped, gait slow and unsteady. His distinguished face was now like a mask of stone. He went into the bedroom and flopped down on the edge of the bed, leaving Stiles and Josie in the front of the house. The sorrow he felt was beyond explanation. Seeing the lifeless bodies of his daughter and Tim would forever be etched in his mind. Then there was David and Meryl Jackson, his longtime friends and Rena's parents. They were gone forever, gunned down like they were nothing. He felt responsible for the death of his daughter, his son-in-law, his dear friends, and basically everything that had happened. He knew she had mental issues, but never did he think she could do something like this.

The pain he felt caused him to question everything. Why did this tragedy have to happen? He tried to live a life pleasing to God, but somehow he must have failed. Margaret had to show up and revealed his past, a past life that he had tried hard to forget over the years.

Pastor felt guilty now that he looked back over how everything went down. He once loved Margaret, adored everything about her. But during those two years they were together, things quickly began to change. Margaret wasn't the same person anymore. He could do nothing to keep her happy. When he got her pregnant he thought their relationship might have a chance, but then she told him she lost their child, and their relationship died too.

After their final break-up, she left Memphis to go back to Chicago where she was originally from, and he established Holy Rock, a long time desire of his heart. He'd been called to preach God's Word when he was a young buck and always had dreams to pastor his own church. At one time, Margaret promised to stand behind him and support his efforts and for a while, a very short while, she would attend church with him. But it wasn't long before she had a change of heart and stopped going altogether.

The day he first encountered Audrey, she walked into Holy Rock, looking fine as ever. He wondered who she was. There was something so enticing about her that he couldn't resist. He soon approached her at their church picnic and the rest was history. He gave in to his flesh and his heart quickly submitted.

Audrey had mentioned that she had a sister, but explained that they did not share the same mother. She did tell him that her sister was schizophrenic and that they did not have a close relationship or any relationship for that matter. During their years of marriage, Audrey never brought her up again and Pastor didn't see the need to either. Now, after all these years, the past had come back to haunt him in a way that was unimaginable.

Pastor forced back the thoughts of the past and in its place thoughts of Sunday's horrid events saturated his mind. He swallowed hard, biting his lips to keep the sobs at bay.

Josie entered and stood motionless in front of him. Her voice was fragile and shaking as she spoke. "Pastor, you should try to get some sleep. It's been a long day. I know it wasn't easy making funeral arrangements, contacting Francesca's friends, and trying to reach out to Rena on top of everything else. But, baby, you have to rest. The next week is going to be tough." She sighed, clasped her slender hands together, and stared at her husband. Tears welled in her eyes.

Pastor looked up at her. A heaviness centered in his chest as he spoke. "I don't know if I *can* sleep, Josie. I don't know how I'm going to move forward from all of this. It's too much, too much to take." Pastor couldn't hold back any longer; wrenching sobs burst forward like a broken dam.

Josie sat on the bed next to him and tried to console him. Her own tears found their way down her cheeks as grief and despair ripped at her heart. She held Pastor against her chest like he was her child instead of her husband. She rocked him back and forth as he wept and cried out to God for mercy.

18

It's amazing that the heart makes no noise when it cracks.
Bliss

Three days had eclipsed since the horrific mass shooting at Holy Rock and Kareena tried calling Stiles again, but like all the previous times, it went to voicemail. She kneeled down and began praying for him and for everyone involved in the horrific tragedy. Stiles had already suffered so much heartbreak and grief in his life. She didn't know how he would ever recover from this one. If the news was accurate, his sister and brother-in-law were among those killed and also the parents of his first ex-wife. She could not begin to imagine, nor did she want to imagine, the pain he must be going through.

After she finished praying, she stood up and went to the tiny space between the family room and the kitchen that she had transformed into her office. It was the perfect space for the built-in desk, chair, her MacBook, and portable printer.

She went online. News continued to trend about the shootings on social media. She read several stories about what happened before she turned the computer off and retreated to her bedroom.

‡

Stiles heard his father weeping in the other room, but he was not in a position to console him. His own grief tormented him by saturating his thoughts of what they'd all been forced to witness at Holy Rock. Having to help Pastor and Josie make funeral arrangements for Francesca only added to Stiles' pain.

To think about how perfect things had gone with the banquet and then the Jubilee service, only to have everything torn apart yet again, was more than he could stomach. He didn't know if there would be any coming back this time around. Death seemed to enjoy wreaking havoc in his life. Over the past five years death had claimed so many people near and dear to him. His mother, his only child, now his sister and brother-in-law, and Mr. and Mrs. Jackson. It made no sense. There was no rhyme or reason to anything anymore. He thought about the scripture in Ecclesiastes...*there is a time for everything, and a season for every activity under the heavens.* He couldn't understand why that passage of scripture would come to mind because he would never believe or accept that this was all part of God's timing. Not the evil that had been perpetrated on innocent people. None of them deserved to be slaughtered.

As he laid back on the bed in the guestroom of his father's house, he questioned his identity. If Margaret was his mother like she claimed, and Audrey took him away from her, then Audrey was not the woman he knew at all. And if Margaret was his mother, he would never get the chance to know the real her because she too, was dead. He was so confused, so messed up in the head.

He looked around the room, the same room he grew up in. Now it felt like a torture chamber because all he seemed to be able to do in this room was cry. His heart was heavy over the thought that in the next few days he would be laying his sister and brother-in-law to rest. Then he would have to travel to Andover to see Rena's parents laid to rest.

"Rena," he said aloud. "Oh, my God, what you must be going through." He searched through his pocket for his phone, pulled it out, and called her. The phone rang until it went to her voicemail. He called again.

"What do you want?"

"Rena, it's Stiles. I was just checking on you. I'm so sorry, Rena," he cried. "I'm just so, so, sorry."

Rena inhaled then slowly released it. "Look, the best thing you can ever do for me is to never ever contact me again. It's because of you and your family that my parents are dead. It's always been some type of mess when it's connected to the Grahams and I hate you, I hate you for everything you've ever done to me," she said, talking slow and low like a zombie.

Stiles mouth hung open. He listened to the words spewing from Rena's mouth. Her biting words only added more hurt on top of what he was already feeling.

Rena was right in her own way. Maybe her life would be different if he hadn't stepped into it. Maybe a lot of people's lives would be better if he or his family hadn't invaded their space.

"Rena, I'm sorry. I can't say it enough. I don't know what else to say. I just wanted you to know that I'm here for you as much as I can be."

"She doesn't need you," the male voice on the phone suddenly interjected. "She has everything she needs. So do like my wife said and stay out of her life," Robert blared over the phone before ending the call.

Stiles felt lower than low. He hated the fact that Rena blamed him and his family for the death of her parents.

"Lord, help Rena get through this tragic time. Help us all, Father God. We need you. I need you. I'm sorry about all of the pain that I've caused in so many people's lives."

His cell phone rang in his hand. He looked at it and saw it was Kareena calling. She'd called several times and had texted him too, but he hadn't responded. His mind was too full of making plans to lay away his sister and brother-in-law. He still had to somehow talk to Hezekiah about the arrangements for Margaret, something he didn't know if he was up to doing or handling. He had to come to terms with what was happening but so far he hadn't done well at all. He continued to hold the phone in his hand and right before the last ring, he answered.

"Hi," he said somberly into the phone.

"Stiles, thank God you answered. How are you?" Kareena asked. You could detect the concern in her voice.

"Not good. Not good at all."

"I've been calling and texting you. I'm so sorry about what happened."

"Thanks."

"Look, I was planning to schedule a flight to Memphis. Since you drove there, I know you don't want to return here by yourself. I mean, under the circumstances and all," she explained. "I can come, attend the funeral services and then I can help you drive back."

"Thanks for offering but I can manage. Just ask the church to pray for me and for my family. I don't know how long I'll be gone. I still have a lot to work out."

"I hate to ask you this, but have you found out if what that woman said is true? Are you really her son and Pastor McCoy's brother?"

"I…haven't had a lot of time to investigate her claims or talk to Hezekiah.

"That's understandable. I'm praying for you."

"Thanks. I'll talk to you later. I'm about to lay it down, try to rest."

"Sure, I understand. And you're right. It's late. You do need to try and get some rest. I know you have a lot going on. Just know that I'm here, Stiles. Please don't shut me out. Okay?"

"Yea. Goodbye, Kareena."

Stiles ended the call and then proceeded to scroll through his contacts in search of Hezekiah's phone number.

Hezekiah lay in the bed next to Fancy. He had finally located Margaret's remaining next of kin who also lived in Chicago. They were horrified to hear what Margaret had done, and also were stunned when Hezekiah told them about himself and Stiles being her sons. The elderly man and woman he located through numbers in Margaret's cell phone said they were Margaret's cousins but they hadn't seen or heard from her in quite some time. Her parents were dead, which he recalled Margaret telling him before he was carted off to prison. The cousins told him they were on fixed incomes and would not be able to offer financial assistance but would try to attend her funeral if their health permitted. Hezekiah refused to let himself get upset over the obvious disinterest they expressed in seeing Margaret laid to rest.

After her body was released by the coroner, Hezekiah made arrangements to have her flown back to Chicago. Hezekiah and Fancy, along with their sons, would travel up there shortly thereafter to funeralize her. He didn't bother to share the details with Stiles because he didn't see a reason to do so. Yes, Margaret said Stiles was her son and his brother, but Hezekiah would have to deal with that truth after he buried her. He had no problem telling Stiles about the arrangements if Stiles came to him. So far that had not been the case.

Hezekiah went to see Margaret in the hospital hours before she passed away. He had a hard time digesting the things Margaret told him on her death bed. He replayed that last conversation over in his head.

"I'm sorry," she mouthed in a low whisper from the hospital bed. She had been shot twice by one or more of the armor bearers; once in her left arm and another bullet entered her stomach. Her heart rate was extremely low, and Hezekiah was told it was only a matter of time before Margaret would succumb to her injuries. Her age played a factor in her dim prognosis combined with the fact that she had pancreatic cancer and a weak heart.

Connected to tubes and machines she struggled to talk. "Horace," she said slowly, calling him by his birth name. "I'm sorry things had to be like this, but I do want you to know that I love you, son."

Hezekiah stood next to her bed and listened. He held her hand as he watched her struggle to breathe through the oxygen mask.

"Please believe me."

"Tell me, are you really my mother?"

"Yes. Yours and Stiles."

"Why? Why couldn't you tell me this when I was a kid. Why now?"

"I did what I thought was best for you. I knew that Tonya loved you just as much as I did and I know you loved her too. She gave you a good home, raised you to love the Lord, all the things that I wasn't mentally able to do. I wanted what was best for you."

"But why, why did you have to kill all those innocent people? You could have just told me the truth. You didn't have to do what you did."

"I felt so hopeless. I guess I wanted your father to pay because I couldn't make Audrey pay. I wanted him to know how much he hurt me. The two of them stole everything from me. I had nothing to lose. Before I came here, I was told that I had no more than four months to live."

"What? Four months?"

"Yes, I was already a dead woman walking with nothing to lose because I already lost everything. I have stage four pancreatic cancer, the same disease Tonya died from."

Hezekiah began to weep. "I'm sorry, so sorry. I just wish you had said all of this a long time ago."

"I know and I'm sorry, but I love you so much. Tell your brother I love him too. Believe me when I say that I didn't mean to hurt either of you. I want you to have a real relationship with him. Promise me that."

Hezekiah slowly nodded in agreement.

"Be the best you can be at Holy Rock. Don't let anyone intimidate you or make you back away from what God has called you to do. You hear me?"

Hezekiah slowly nodded again.

"Now that you know the truth I want you to make Chauncey Graham pay. All this is his fault. If he had only listened to me when I told him I was pregnant with you, but he wouldn't. He didn't want you and he didn't want me." Margaret pushed the automatic pain medication at her side and shortly after closed her eyes. The strong medication rendered her unconscious.

Hezekiah remained standing by her side until Fancy walked into the ICU room and took hold of his hand. She leaned against his shoulder and held him around his waist. When she heard him exhale, she took it as a sign that it was time to leave. She gently guided her husband away from Margaret's bedside and led him out of the room. One hour later. Alone. Margaret died.

19

"Everybody's journey is individual. James Baldwin

Several weeks after the Holy Rock Massacre, the dead had been laid to rest and life continued, not standing still for anyone. The tally from the massacre included seven dead, eleven people wounded, three of them with serious but non-life threatening injuries and eight with minor injuries which included Xavier. Xavier experienced no residual complaints or problems from the flesh wound in his left arm. He was more traumatized than anything, having been in the midst of the shootings. He was thankful that his life had been spared.

Trying to get back to normal, he and Raymone, had plans to go check out a movie they'd both wanted to see. It was a rare occasion, but Fancy agreed to let him drive, so he scooped up Raymone and they headed to the movie theatre.

Xavier and Raymone had been friends ever since Raymone started at Holy Rock Upper School. Raymone was a year younger but they were both seniors. Neither of them wanted anyone to know that they were engaged in a homosexual relationship.

Xavier started having feelings for the same sex when he was in eighth grade. He didn't know what brought it on, only that instead of finding himself attracted to girls, he was more interested in boys, and often fantasized about being in a relationship with one. He knew what he had been taught all of his life about homosexuality, that it was wrong and a sin. But he still couldn't keep his feelings at bay. So he hid them as much as he could. He talked to girls occasionally, got a phone number every now and then, and as he grew older and started dating, he took a few of them out, but he didn't feel that spark, didn't want to take it any farther than a meal or a movie and being platonic friends.

When he met Raymone, he felt an immediate attraction and it wasn't long before he realized that Raymone was battling the same homosexual demons. They never openly talked about their sexual preferences; it went unsaid. They had never crossed the line with each other sexually, but they made out ever chance they got.

Unlike Xavier, Raymone's parents and siblings knew about his homosexuality and loved and accepted him for who he was. It was the main reason that Xavier felt comfortable whenever he was at Raymone's house. The whole family treated him like he was a normal kid and didn't pass judgment on him.

Raymone's father talked to Xavier when he arrived to pick up Raymone for the movie. "Xavier, son, do you mind if I talk to you for a minute."

"Of course, sir."

"Follow me," Raymone's father said.

Xavier joined him outside on the patio.

"I want to know that while we don't condone homosexuality, we accept Raymone for who he is, and we love him unconditionally. By the same token, whenever you are in our home we want you to feel welcome. I want you to know that me or my wife, or Raymone's siblings, will never disclose anything to anyone outside of this home. Do you understand?"

"Yes, sir. And thank you, thank you for that."

"I still think you should sit down and talk to your parents," he told Xavier. "It will eat away at you until you do, son."

"Yes, sir. I know. It just never seems like the right time. Plus, I don't know what my parents will say or do. My dad preaches about homosexuality all the time." Xavier looked away, pushed his black framed designer eyeglasses up on his nose, and hooked one elbow over the backrest of his chair. "He makes sure his congregation knows that the Bible says it's a sin. I don't want to shame my dad or my mother. But I just want to be me."

"God understands, and if your father is truly a man of God, which I believe that he is, then he won't judge you. Now he may not agree with your choice but that doesn't mean that he won't love you just the same. There's a lot of misconception about how Christians look at people who are gay or lesbian. They think we hate homosexuals, and that's so far from the truth. Again, I don't like the fact that Raymone, and you, are gay, but I love my son and I would die for him if I had to. Do you understand where I'm coming from?"

"Yes, sir. Thanks for the advice, and for understanding," Xavier said. He looked over his shoulder and saw Raymone standing at the patio door.

"When you're done talking, come to my room so we can finish up our game before we leave for the movies."

"I'm done talking, son. You can go," he said, patting Xavier on his shoulder. "But just know that if you ever need someone to talk to, I'm here," Raymone's father assured him.

Xavier and Raymone spent some time playing Elder Scrolls then turned their attention online to one of the sites they frequented. They engaged in conversation via private messenger with other gay teens and young adults.

"Now that you've talked to my dad, what do you think about telling your parents that you're gay?" asked Raymone.

"I don't know. But I probably won't do it anytime soon. Too much has been going on. I don't want to make things worse by coming out now."

"I know, but I'm just saying, the longer you wait the harder it's going to be."

"Your parents are way different than mine. They're cool with you being gay, but my parents are not like that. They're going to stuff the Bible down my throat and I don't want to deal with that."

"Have it your way, but I'm just saying, you still need to tell 'em sooner or later."

"Yeah, it'll be later then...much later."

"I hear ya. Well, let's shut this down and get outta here. The movie starts in an hour."

"I'm with ya."

"Mom...Dad, we're leaving," Raymone shouted as he and Xavier headed to the front door.

His mother appeared. "You boys be safe out there. And Xavier, drive carefully. You don't want the police to have any excuse to pull you over. Enough of our black boys are being murdered and locked up as it is, all for no reason. But remember what I told you both. If the police do stop you, make sure you let him know beforehand every move you are about to make. If he asks for your driver's license and registration, tell him where it is and then tell him when you are about to pull out your license and when you're reaching for your registration. Don't make any sudden moves. You understand?"

"Yes, ma'am," Xavier said followed by Raymone.

The teens walked outside to Xavier's car parked on the curb in front of Raymone's house. The night air was breezy but warm for a fall night. Stars sparkled and you could hear a dog or two barking in the neighborhood.

"Your parents are straight," Xavier said as the friends approached Xavier's car.

"Yeah, they aight."

"Mane, I wish I could talk to my parents like you talk to yours. But I already know how they'll react. Especially my dad."

"Yeah, I hear ya. But at some point they're going to start wondering why you don't have a girlfriend, you know?"

"Yeah they're already asking that. My brother too. I got to tell 'em. I don't know when or how."

"You'll figure it out. For now, don't sweat it. Let's go check out this movie and have a good time. You feel me?"

"Yeah, I feel ya."

20

*Family is supposed to be our safe haven. Most often it's
the place where we find the deepest heartache.*
Iyanla Vanzant

After walking on the river and strolling along Beale
Street, Khalil and Dee dined at the restaurant B.B. Kings.
They listened to some blues band and chatted while they
waited on their food.

"I hope you've enjoyed your birthday so far," Dee told
Khalil."

"Thanks, I have." He eyed his wrist again and smiled
at the expensive timepiece Dee had gifted him.

"So, you have a three-year old kid, huh?"

"Yes. His name is Elijah." Dee scrolled through the
pictures on her cell phone until she arrived at the various
pictures of her son. She proceeded to show Khalil
pictures of the boy.

"Why don't I ever see him around?"

"He lives mostly with his father and his wicked
stepmother."

"Umm, I take it you two don't get along, huh?

"That's an understatement. But my kid seems to like
her."

"How do you feel about that?" questioned Khalil.

Dee shrugged. "It is what it is."

"And you were married to Stiles Graham," Khalil
grimaced.

"Yes, I sure was. I find it hilarious now."

"Why is that?" asked Khalil.

"Well, come on now. Can you picture me as the First
Lady?" Dee laughed.

Khalil chuckled. "I bet you were an awesome First Lady," Khalil said, leaning in and kissing Dee on the lips.

"I don't think your uncle would agree."

"He's not my uncle. I don't care what my Aunt Margaret said before she died. It's all so crazy. I'm just glad everything is over. Hey, let me ask you something."

"Sure. What?"

"You were part of their family at one time so why didn't you go to his sister's funeral? Was it because you didn't want to see him or what?"

"I don't want any dealings with Stiles, with any of the Grahams for that matter. They're all a bunch of fake, lying hypocrites. You, of all people, should know that after hearing what your aunt, uhhh, your grandmother...anyway, after hearing what she said. I always knew that family was up to no good. Stiles was always quick to condemn other people when he should be the last one to talk."

"I hear ya."

"Have your father and the Grahams talked yet? I wonder what it's going to mean for your family and theirs now that y'all are supposed to be related."

"They're supposed to be meeting up sometime next week. It took a while for everyone to digest the news. My dad isn't too happy knowing that his biological father didn't want anything to do with him or Aunt Margaret. That's sad, mane. How can dude have a son, knows he has a son, and then raise somebody else's kid but has nothing to do with his own flesh and blood. I used to respect Reverend Graham but now that I see what kind of man he really is, all respect is gone. I hate guys like him who do all that religious talk but then their own house is messed up."

"Yea, I'm sorry for what your father must be going through. And the fact that he didn't get the chance to know his mother as his mother, that's sad. And to have a daddy that was more than a deadbeat, the man actually chose not to be in his life."

"Yeah, fa sho. But look, we're supposed to be celebrating my birthday. I don't want to spend any more time talking about my family drama."

"I'm sorry. I didn't mean to pry."

"You are not prying, but since we're speaking of family, I want you to come to a birthday dinner my family is having for me this Saturday. My mom always makes a big deal out of our birthdays. She loves any reason to entertain. There won't be many people there, just a few close friends. You in?"

"Uhhh, I don't know, Khalil. I don't want to ruin your family's time with you. I mean, what are they going to say about you seeing me? And when they find out that I'm Stiles' ex-wife, among other things," she said, clearing her throat, "everything will hit the fan."

"You mean to tell me that you're worried about what other people think? Come on now, not you. Not Lady Dee." Khalil chuckled. "I want you there. Don't deny me."

"I'll think about it, okay? But I won't make any promises."

"Cool. But you better believe I'm going to do everything I possibly can to persuade you," he said leaning in again and this time nibbling on her neck and earlobe.

"Khalil, you're going to start something."

"Exactly what I'm trying to do," he teased.

The server brought their food to the table.

"Let's eat and get out of here so I can give you your *real* birthday present." Dee laughed then took a bite of her food.

"Umm, I can't wait," Khalil said, biting into his smoked beef brisket burger.

‡

"Dang, girl. You look like you just stepped off of a magazine cover." The image before him made him want to drool.

Being that money was no object for her, Dee had shelled out big bucks for the black Valentino embroidered-tulle cocktail dress with a jewel neckline. She looked stunning. She was set on looking beautiful and elegant. It didn't matter that she was only going to the McCoy's house and not some ultra-exclusive place. From what she already knew about Fancy and Hezekiah, they were flashy people who loved everything that money could buy so she wanted to look better than her best. Khalil didn't impress her as that type but she spared no expense on him. The timepiece she preferred to call it that she bought him for his birthday cost her a couple of grand, but it meant nothing to Dee. She believed in sparing no expense when it came to something she wanted, and she wanted Khalil.

She hadn't told her sister, Brooke, about him yet, and had no plans on telling her or her parents that she was seeing someone again. For now, it wasn't their business. If the relationship between her and Khalil turned serious then maybe it would be her turn to take him around her family, but until then, she was content on things being as they were.

"Thank you, baby. I want to make a good impression." Dee smiled.

"Forget my family; you've made your point and from what you've told me, you all already know each other quite well."

"True. Fancy and I worked closely together when I was the first lady. And Pastor McCoy, well let's just say, he came through for me when I lost my baby girl. I owe him a lot. But it's a whole other subject when they find out that I'm sleeping with their son."

"You know something?"

"What?"

"You're impressing me so much right now that I'm thinking we should stay here and have our own private celebration." Khalil walked up to her and grabbed her into his arms and kissed her feverishly.

"Khalil, stop it. You're going to mess up my makeup."

"I can't help it. I can't get enough of you."

"You are just going to have to control yourself. After we leave your birthday dinner, we'll come back here or go christen your new apartment."

"Yea, I like that idea." Khalil smiled, took hold of Dee by her waist and they set out to go to his parents' house.

Khalil pulled up and parked behind several cars already at his parents' house. He went to the passenger's side and opened the door for his lovely lady. Maybe they hadn't been seeing each other for very long, but Khalil liked her. He really, really liked her. She was smart, funny, sexy and let's not forget rich. Just his cup of tea.

He extended his hand and helped Dee get out of the car. She placed her handbag on her paralyzed side, extended her other hand out toward Khalil, and stepped out of the car. She had no idea what the McCoys would have to say about their twenty-one year old son bringing home a thirty-six year old woman, especially one whose name was Detria Graham. She smiled at the thought.

"What are you smiling about, pretty lady?" asked Khalil.

"Oh, just thinking about how your parents are going to react when they see me."

"Hey, we aren't going down that road again. It is what it is. You're with me and either they deal with it or they don't. If they make you feel anyways uncomfortable, just give me that look and we're out. You got it?"

"Yeah, I got it."

Khalil rang the doorbell then proceeded to try to open the front door, but it was locked.

"I've got it," Fancy yelled from the other side and within seconds, the door was opened. "Baby, I knew it was you." She laughed but immediately froze when she saw the woman holding on to her son's arm.

Khalil leaned in and kissed his mom on the cheek and proceeded to walk into the house. He stopped, turned and closed the door.

"Mama, you remember Dee, right?" He squeezed Dee's hand tighter and Fancy noticed the affectionate gesture right away.

Fancy was at a loss for words to see Detria Graham after all this time, but she was even more perturbed that she was obviously messing around with her son.

"What in God's name are you doing here? And with my son?" Fancy demanded. It was apparent that seeing Detria with Khalil did not make her a happy camper.

"Mom, don't start. Dee is my guest."

Ignoring her son, she continued in on Detria. "My God, how could you? Have you no morals? You're the same age as me if not older! You ought to be ashamed of yourself."

"Fancy, please. I'm not going to go there with you. It's Khalil's birthday. Surely, you aren't going to ruin it by being petty," Detria said, waving her off.

"Being petty? Are you serious? Can't you find someone your own age? Oh, I forgot. I'm sure they know your history of being a tramp."

"Mom, I said stop it!"

"Khalil doesn't have a problem with me, so I don't see why you should."

"Because he's a kid, for God's sake," Fancy exclaimed.

"Fancy, have you looked at your son lately. He's all man." She looked at Khalil and then stood on her toes to kiss him on his cheek. "I'm hardly taking advantage of him. It may be the other way around," she purred.

Fancy balled her fists, pursed her lips, and prepared to lunge at Detria, but Khalil intervened.

"Mom, don't!" He jumped in between the two of them. "Dee's right. I'm not a kid. I'm a grown man, and she's my date and my lady. If you can't respect that, then I'm sorry, we'll just have to leave."

Dee smiled wickedly at Fancy and held on to Khalil even tighter.

"Have it your way, but this isn't over, Detria," she said angrily. She didn't want to ruin Khalil's evening with a bunch of uncivilized antics. Enough craziness had already gone on in the family with Margaret's insanity and she wanted her family to have an evening of fun.

"Khalil, most of the guests are already here and gathered in the living room and outside. Everyone is excited to join in your birthday tribute." She looped her arm into Khalil's and gently tugged just enough to break the hold Khalil had on Dee's hand. "Oh, guess what? I almost forgot to tell you."

"Tell me what, Ma?"

Fancy stopped and smiled. "Tori is here. She arrived yesterday from New York. Isn't that nice?" Fancy and Dee's eyes met and both women gave each other a fake smile.

"Is that right?" Khalil appeared agitated then looked at Dee, smiled, took hold of her hand again, and walked toward the living room.

The living room held a custom made oak table that seated twelve. The room had slide away pocket glass doors that opened out and into an outdoor space with plenty of extra seating. There was a lanai, full kitchen, grill and a huge mounted television.

"Who is Tori? An ex-girlfriend, I suppose?" Dee whispered as they entered the living room.

"Yeah, something like that. But you don't have anything to be concerned about."

"Khalil, I'm not some jealous little college girl. Jealousy is not who I am, especially not over some youngster."

Khalil looked at Dee and smiled proudly.

As the couple walked further into the living room, people were standing around talking, sipping on cocktails, and dining on hors d'oeuvres. Several guests stopped what they were doing to greet Khalil and began extending happy birthday wishes.

A beautiful, slender, shapely young woman with long, coal black, curly hair approached and immediately greeted Khalil with a deep kiss. "Happy birthday," she said, not bothering to look at Dee or acknowledge her presence.

Dee wanted to belt the girl, but being the woman she was, she maintained her composure.

"Thanks, Tori," he said while simultaneously pushing her back and away.

Khalil and Tori met at Holy Rock when he first came to Memphis, and the two of them hit it off. They started hanging out with friends then the two of them started hanging around each other. He liked her but he wasn't ready to be exclusive. The only thing on his mind and in his sight after getting out of juvenile detention and moving to Memphis was hooking up with as many girls as he could.

Everything blew up when only a few short months into their relationship, she told him she was pregnant. He chastised himself for not taking his father's advice to always, always, always strap up.

There was one thing about his father that made their relationship special and that was he was easy to talk to. Khalil regretted that he failed to take advantage of that and instead started hanging around with the wrong crowd and indulging in heavy drug usage. That's when everything in his family went downhill fast. Before he knew it, he was getting into all sorts of trouble back in Chicago. He didn't realize it until later just how blessed he was to still be alive when hundreds of murders were reported every day in the Windy City.

Khalil went to his dad when Tori told him she was pregnant and Hezekiah immediately told his son to go talk to Tori and tell her that the best thing for them to do was for her to get an abortion. Yes, he was a man of the cloth, but his son was not ready to be a father so Hezekiah gave him worldly advice rather than Godly advice. If any of his pastor constituents knew that he was telling his own kid to kill another human being, Hezekiah imagined the flack he would receive. But no one knew what went on behind the huge oak doors of the McCoys and it was nobody's business as far as Hezekiah was concerned.

"You have to tell her that she has her whole life ahead of her, son. And so do you. She's about to graduate from high school and leave for college, and she told you that she was supposed to go study abroad her first year, right?"

"Yes, sir," Khalil told his father, worried.

"Having a baby would end all of that. And you, well, son, you are working in the church and I told you if you keep doing the excellent job that you're doing even greater things can happen for you. Having a kid will put a hold on all of that. It's a lot of responsibility. And you don't plan to spend the rest of your life with Tori, do you?"

"Heck no. I'm not ready to be with one girl. I like her but not enough to settle down and make her or anyone else wifey. No way."

Hezekiah patted his son on his shoulder. "Believe me, son, I feel where you're coming from. That's why you have to talk to her. Don't make her mad and don't make her feel like you want things to end between the two of you. Once you convince her to have an abortion, then you break things off with her. But not until you're sure she went through with it. You hear me?"

"Yes, sir."

"Here," Hezekiah said, going into his pocket and retrieving his wallet. "This ought to cover the expenses. He gave Khalil several hundred dollar bills. "Let me know if you need more. Do you want me to find a doctor who can perform the abortion?"

"Uh, sure."

"Okay, you talk to Tori. I'll get with George and he'll find out who the best doctor will be. I want to make sure this is done quickly and discreetly. I don't even want your mother to know about it. You understand? You know she's close to Tori's mother. Plus, they are faithful members of Holy Rock. I don't want to ruin that."

Khalil understood the term 'faithful members.' That meant that they shelled out their fair share of money to the church. "Yes, sir, and thanks, Dad," Khalil said with a somber look on his face.

"Hey, everything is going to be all right, son. No need for the gloomy look."

True to his word, after Khalil convinced Tori that it would be the best thing for them at the time, Hezekiah arranged everything behind the scenes for the girl to have an abortion.

A week after she had the abortion, following Hezekiah's advice, Khalil broke things off with Tori. She was hurt but she left to study abroad and Hezekiah couldn't have been more relieved. As a going away gift, Hezekiah blessed the girl with twenty-five hundred dollars.

Hezekiah wasn't especially overjoyed to see Tori and her parents at Khalil's birthday dinner, but he knew Fancy would invite them because Fancy and Tori's mother were friends outside of church. Tori's parents were both successful engineers and they paid well above and beyond their tithes and offerings. Hezekiah was not about to do anything that might ruin that.

Dee watched as Tori disappeared down the hall. Khalil was busy talking to the guests so it was ample time for her to excuse herself and follow Tori. She watched as the young girl entered the bathroom and before she could close it behind her, Dee pushed herself in and locked the door.

"What are you doing?" Tori asked, looking alarmed.

"Look, let's get something straight, little girl. I am not the one to play with. You do that crap with some of your little college friends, or whoever."

Tori looked a little frightened but still managed to smirk. "Sounds like someone is a little J. Honey, no need to worry your *old* little self," she mocked. "I've been there done that. I have no interest in Khalil anymore."

Dee almost lost control when Tori called her old. She wanted to lay hands on her and not in the way they did in church.

"You may be able to tell yourself that lie, but I know better. So, like I said. Don't mess with me. You stay away from Khalil, or you will be sorry. Very, very sorry." Dee turned around and walked out the bathroom as quickly as she had barged in, leaving Tori's heart beating like it was about to pop out of her chest.

Going back to the living room, Dee met Fancy as she walked toward her. "I can't believe I'm saying this, but everything is quite nice," she said to Fancy.

"Cut the crap. What do you want with Khalil? If you think for one minute that he is serious about you then you're more than just a fool, you're an old fool. You should be looking for a trick your own age."

"Excuse me?" said Dee.

"You heard me."

Dee was not one to be intimidated especially by the likes of Fancy McCoy. She stood her ground. "Baby, if you think I'm going anywhere, you are sadly mistaken. Now try me if you want to, First Lady Fancy McCoy," she said, getting up close in Fancy's personal space. "Or better yet, ask Stiles...or your husband about me. They'll tell you that I'm not one to be messed with," she seethed.

Dee strutted off, leaving Fancy standing in the hall, her face flushed with anger and confusion.

Hezekiah listened and watched out of sight from around the corner. Like his wife, he was surprised to see Khalil with Detria Graham, of all people. He wondered where they could have met and what had attracted her to him. Detria was an attractive and shapely woman, so he understood why Khalil would be infatuated with her, but why on God's green earth would she want to hook up with a young boy like Khalil? He would wait until the perfect time and ask her that question himself.

Hezekiah stepped back and went into the kitchen. He would have a talk with Khalil later.

"Nice affair," George said, walking up on Hezekiah in the kitchen, a smugness plastered on his rugged face. "You have quite the array of guests here this evening. Quite intriguing."

"Yes, I guess you could say that."

"It's a good thing the First Lady invited me and Bernice, don't you think?"

Hezekiah gave George his full attention. "And what's that supposed to mean?"

"It means that from the looks of some of your guests this is the perfect setting for a lot of drama to take place." He scanned the room with his eyes. "Seems that I might need to keep my eyes wide open. Anything can happen tonight." George lifted his glass of bourbon to his lips, gave a shrug and was gone, leaving Hezekiah with a cold, hard-eyed expression.

George Reeves and his wife, Bernice, were among the carefully selected guests invited to attend Khalil's birthday dinner. George enjoyed his life of retirement more than his wife could ever imagine. Hezekiah paid him well to keep his mouth shut about his past and about his present day activities too. He made sure Hezekiah's secret was safe and that no one, especially Fancy, would discover that Pastor McCoy had a mistress and leased a luxury condo in downtown Memphis. In addition, he promised to keep secret his knowledge of the ton of money Hezekiah skimmed from the church that helped fund his extracurricular lifestyle.

Fancy had no real knowledge that not long after becoming Senior Pastor of Holy Rock Hezekiah had returned to his old ways. He was sticking his hands in Holy Rock's cookie jar in every possible way one could imagine. He didn't pass up any chance to line his pockets with the tons of money pouring into Holy Rock. His love offering was more than enough for them to live off, but the extra he padded his pockets with took him well into being able to live the life he always dreamed of. As long as George remained on his side, he believed that his secret life was safe. If things became iffy or uncertain, he could count on George to make his problems disappear.

George would remain loyal to him as long as Hezekiah remained loyal to him by making sure he received payment as a Holy Rock employee and as long as Hezekiah kept the under-the-table money flowing. His former dislike for the church had changed and now he was always eager to be at Holy Rock, if only for his own self-serving purpose.

As George exited the kitchen and headed outside to join his wife and some of the other guests, he saw Xavier and his friend go up the stairs. George's detective instinct sensed that there was something weird about Hezekiah's baby boy, so this was the perfect time to follow the teens and see what they were up to. He couldn't put behind his

Shelia E. Bell

days of being a detective and the McCoys always gave him plenty to keep the fire blazing over his cop days.

Quietly, he followed them upstairs. He watched as they disappeared behind the door into what he supposed was Xavier's room. Looking around to make sure no one else was behind him, George eased in closer and positioned himself on the side of the door that they left slightly ajar. Xavier must have thought he closed it all the way, but thanks to George's good luck, he hadn't. What he witnessed almost made him blow his cover. He saw the two boys display affection toward each other that was altogether against everything he believed. He felt sickened by the sight. He pulled out his phone and took several pictures before he shook his head and walked quietly back down the stairs.

Ahhh, more ammunition to add to my arsenal, he thought. He returned to the party, had himself another stiff drink, sat down outside and chilled. His days of being an ex-cop and a faithful, church going member were paying off better than he could have ever hoped or expected.

21

*Double double, toil and trouble, fire burn
and cauldron trouble.* Wm. Shakespeare

"You ready, son?" Pastor said to Stiles.

"Yes, sir. Let's go see how we can resolve this issue
between the McCoys and the Grahams. I know it's been
troubling you ever since Margaret said what she said and
did what she did."

"It's been three weeks since Margaret went on that
rampage, and my mind is nowhere close to being at
peace. This Sunday will be the first time back at Holy
Rock, and that's only if I can resolve things with
Hezekiah." Pastor lowered his head. "I have so much to
make up for, son."

"Pastor, you've always told me that what's done in
the dark always comes to light. This is one of those
things. Now that your past has been exposed, it's time
you take hold of the reins and do what it takes to fix
things. God is in control. We may not understand
everything that He's allowed to happen, but being men of
faith, we have to be strong and trust in Him."

"You are so right, son. But I hate that it took losing
my daughter and son-in-law in the process. They didn't
deserve to die. It's more than my heart can stand. And the
Jacksons, well that's another open wound that I don't
know if time can ever heal. Knowing that Rena blames us
for the death of her parents is something I will never be
able to live down. I don't blame her for feeling the way
that she does, but it's just hard, son. They were my
friends. This whole thing is more than this old man can
take."

"Pastor, you're a strong man. God has seen you through some trying times. It's hard losing Francesca, but I know that the both of us have to try our best to keep moving. I mean, it's certainly beyond our comprehension but the word of God says he will give us beauty for our ashes. He will strengthen and uphold us."

"I know God's word better than many. But it just hurts so bad. First, your mother, then my precious little grandbaby, and now my daughter. I feel like Job must have felt."

"You can't give up now, Pastor. Come on, let's get going."

Pastor walked back to the entrance of the kitchen where Josie was making a pitcher of fresh lemonade. He walked over to where she stood and kissed her on the side of her face affectionately. "I'll be back as soon as I can," he told her.

"Chauncey, everything is going to turn out fine. I've prayed and asked the Lord to order your steps and Pastor McCoy's too."

"Thank you, baby,

Arriving at Hezekiah's house, Pastor had no idea what he would say to the man who was his son. How could he begin to justify his absence in his life? He had played everything over in his mind. The past weeks of laying his loved ones and friends to rest had taken precedence over everything that Margaret exposed. This evening, however, was inevitable. He had to face the music.

"Come in," Fancy invited when she opened the door to Pastor and Stiles. It was hard to read her demeanor. She didn't seem overly excited or pleased to see either of them. "Hezekiah is in his office. He'll be out in a minute.

Please," she escorted them into the family room, "have a seat in the family room."

"Thank you, Sister McCoy," Pastor said followed by Stiles.

She left them in the family room and Hezekiah appeared just as they were taking their seats.

"Good afternoon," Hezekiah said. He had been looking forward to this meeting with Pastor for a few days, and not exactly in a good way. He wanted to see what reason this man would give for choosing not to be in his life when he was a kid. For Hezekiah, there was nothing Pastor could tell him that would justify his absence.

"Good afternoon, Hezekiah," Stiles and Pastor said almost simultaneously.

Hezekiah walked into the center of the room, folded his arms, and stopped. "You know, I have done some shameful things in my life. All of which I am sorry for. But I chalk it up to growing up in Cabrini-Green, having the only man I've ever known as father gunned down, and witnessing the hustle most of my life." His expression was hard and his voice full of bitterness. "But one thing my mother always instilled in me, God rest her soul, and I'm talking about the woman who raised me as her own. One thing she told me was that God is the answer to every situation, every problem, and every need. She told me to rely on him and to put my trust in him. She took me and my brother to church every time the church doors opened. She and my daddy kept us safe, kept us fed and clothed. All that time, I thought she was my mother and that my daddy was my real father. What kid grows up thinking that his parents are not really his parents? But to find out at this stage in my life that all of what I grew up

Shelia E. Bell

believing was a lie. Can you even imagine how that makes me feel?"

"Heze…

"Shut up!" Hezekiah yelled. "I'm talking. I don't want to hear your sorry excuses."

"Hold up, man," Stiles angrily interjected. He didn't like the fact that this dude had flipped out on Pastor.

"You don't tell me to hold up. I'm only getting started. I have a lot more to say!"

"It's okay, Stiles. Let him have his say."

"You're darn right I'm going to have my say. You wanted this meeting so bad. Well, you got it. You've been standing up in a pulpit calling yourself preaching God's word, and all the time you're living a lie. Here I am, thinking I was unworthy, but you, you take the cake. How could you raise this dude," he pointed at Stiles, "as your own son but turn your back on me, your own flesh and blood son?"

"Hezekiah, I don't blame you for being angry. And I can't tell you anything, except the truth. That truth is I didn't know I had a son. At first Margaret told me she was pregnant, and I was thrilled at the prospect of having a kid. I thought we could possibly work things out so we could raise our child together, but it didn't end up like that. Your mother and I just couldn't get along so I decided that it was best if we called things off. I promised her that I would be in my kid's life and she said she was fine with that. But a few days later, she told me she lost our baby through a miscarriage. I was hurt to hear that but I had no reason to doubt what she said. With no future for us, she decided to pack up her things and go back to Chicago and I hadn't heard from her since. And as for being Audrey's sister and Audrey stealing Stiles

140

from her, I had no idea about that either. You have to believe me. Margaret was unstable—"

"Don't you even try it. Don't blame this on her. She's not here to defend herself, but she told me a lot, the whole story before she took her last breath. And you, you knew you had a kid, a son. Me...I have two sons. I can't imagine turning my back on either of them and pretending like they never existed. But you, you seemed to find it easy and now you want to blame my mother. At least Aunt Margaret made sure I was with people who loved me and cared about me. At least she remained a part of my life, a valuable part at that. But you, you're nothing but a lying coward. You're sitting up in my house with him and the both of you ain't worth a dime. I don't care if you are supposed to be my brother. Tonya's son is more of a brother to me than you will ever be."

"I'm telling you, if I knew I had a son, you have to believe that I would have been in your life."

"What I have to say to you is that I want you out of the pulpit at Holy Rock. I want you out of my life. I don't want to see you, deal with you or you," he said angrily, looking from Pastor to Stiles.

"Son."

"Don't call me your son. My father is dead."

"Hezekiah, baby, please calm down," Fancy said, entering the family room after hearing her husband explode in a fit of rage.

"You can't put him out of the church," Stiles stood and spoke.

"And who says I can't?"

"What right do you have to do that? Okay, so he wasn't in your life when you were growing up, but that's in the past. There's nothing anyone can do about it. What matters is now. The present, Hezekiah. You're a grown man, not some little kid. Get over it and move forward. All of us see just how fleeting life really is after what we've gone through these past weeks. And what about forgiveness?"

"Look, man," Hezekiah said, walking up closer to Stiles. "Who are you to tell me what to think or what to feel or what to say? You were raised by this man who should have been raising me. Now he wants to sit up in here and tell me that what Margaret said wasn't the truth, and that he didn't know about me. Bull! So step back or get out of my house."

"Pastor, I'll be outside. Take your time, but I need to get out of here before things turn ugly."

"You got that right," Hezekiah hissed.

"Hezekiah, Stiles, please don't fight. Stiles, don't leave. I have this to say and I'll leave your house," Pastor pleaded.

Pastor took Hezekiah's silence as permission to speak.

"I didn't come here to fight. I came to say that I'm sorry," Pastor said, confused about what to call his own son. "All I can say about what happened is that I was young, stupid, and I made a lot of mistakes. And I'm sorry. But believe me when I tell you that I didn't know about you. But you're also right; I shouldn't blame Margaret. She was sick and not responsible for her deranged actions, so I can't blame anyone but myself. But asking me to leave the church that I founded, I don't understand why you would even want to do something like that. You're a man of God just like we are," he continued, looking up next to him at Stiles. "You know how important the ministry is to me. I'm not a young man anymore, Hezekiah. I don't know how much longer the good Lord is going to keep me around."

"Don't play that sorry song and dance tune with me. My mother is dead, the woman who raised me is dead, the man who raised me is dead, and you, you're still around here kicking and breathing talking about you made a mistake! There is no way Margaret would lie about you on her death bed. How could you try to destroy her by lying on her now? I have no respect for you, man. None whatsoever, so you can miss me with all your empty words."

Pastor stood up next to Stiles with the face and stance of a broken man.

Stiles spoke forcefully. "Look, I know this is a lot to digest, but it's still no need to come down on him like this."

Hezekiah released a hearty laugh. "Fancy, do you hear this fool?"

Fancy leaned in and whispered, "Baby, please. I told you, you need to calm down."

Xavier came downstairs, preparing to leave for practice for the upcoming school play that Holy Rock Upper School was putting on in the next several weeks. He stopped to listen when he heard his father's booming voice. He knew right away that someone had made him mad. He walked closer to the family room, peeped around the corner, and saw Pastor Graham and the man who was supposed to be his father's younger brother. He felt that it had to be hard on his dad finding out in such a horrific way about his birth father and brother.

Xavier continued to listen a little longer until his phone notified him that he had a text message. He looked at it. It was from Raymone.

"You still scooping me up or nah?"

"Yeah, b ther n 15," Xavier texted back.

Shelia E. Bell

The teens were going to participate in the school's senior play and had practice today. Stepping from around the corner and making himself visible, Xavier interrupted the heated discussion.

"Excuse me."

Hezekiah stopped talking and everyone turned toward the sound of Xavier's voice.

"Hello, Xavier," Pastor said.

"Hi, Pastor Graham. Hello, sir," he then looked and addressed Stiles. "Ma...Dad, just wanted to let you know that I'm about to leave for drama practice."

Fancy walked toward her son. "Okay, but please come straight home after practice."

"Cut the boy some slack, Fancy," Hezekiah ordered. "Be careful out there, son."

"Yes, sir," he said and then proceeded to leave with Fancy trailing behind him like a puppy dog.

When they disappeared out of the family room, Hezekiah continued. "Look, I think I've made myself clear, so let's just say this little meet and greet is done."

Hezekiah walked past Pastor and Stiles. As he walked out, Fancy walked back up, "Fancy, baby, do me a favor and show them the door."

22

Being able to wait is a sign of true love and patience. Anyone can say I love you but not everyone can wait and prove it's true. Unknown

Stiles zipped through his playlist until he found the perfect song that would help to give him some inner peace as he made the drive back to Houston. He'd been on the road for a little over an hour but it felt like hours. It had been six weeks since he'd stood in the pulpit of his own church and it was time he got back to Full of Grace to tend his flock.

As he listened to "Better" by Hezekiah Walker, his mind began to transform from dwelling on all that had happened over the span of six weeks to a deep spiritual tranquility. His spirit told him that everything would be fine because the God he served was still in control. He continued listening to his playlists of tunes until his phone started ringing, turning off the music.

"Hi, Kareena," Stiles said into his Bluetooth.

"Hey, how are you?" she asked.

"Glad to be headed back that way."

Kareena smiled. She was glad that Stiles had finally made the decision to return to Houston. She understood that he had business to handle and things to settle in Memphis, but she missed him and his congregation missed him too.

"I was checking in on you. How much longer before you get here?"

"I still have about four and a half hours to go. Should be there say around six thirty or seven. I was going to stop and get something to eat but I changed my mind. I'm going to try to push on straight through. I'll get something when I make it there."

"I don't mind preparing something for you. I'll fry you some chicken. I know that's your favorite."

"You don't have to do that. Why don't we plan on going out and grabbing something when I get there? And in case I haven't mentioned it before now, I do miss you."

Kareena was glad Stiles couldn't see her blushing. "It's good to be missed," she said. "Anyway, I was just calling so I'll see you in a few hours. Be safe. Talk to you later."

"Yeah, talk to you later."

Kareena was a nice woman who Stiles believed would make someone a good wife one day. Stiles didn't want to even think that his feelings might grow that deeply for her. He didn't want to mess up someone else's life like he'd messed up his own.

Stiles called to check in on Pastor and Josie after he finished talking to Kareena. Pastor still wasn't fairing too well and was really at an all-time low now that Hezekiah banned him from Holy Rock. A piece of his heart had been ripped apart and the pain was unbearable. Stiles could hear the hurt in his father's voice when he talked to him, but there was nothing he could do to change things because Hezekiah didn't want anything to do with him either. Several times since their meeting, he had tried calling and texting Hezekiah hoping he could convince him to look at things differently, but Hezekiah refused to talk to him, so Stiles prayed that the state of depression would be lifted from Pastor and that Hezekiah would find it in his heart to forgive him.

Next, after talking to Pastor and Josie for about ten minutes, he dialed Rena's number. He didn't expect her to answer, and she didn't, but he prayed that she would. Rena was right about one thing Stiles admitted to himself - ever since she had been connected to his family, she had gone through a lot of emotional heartbreak. She hadn't deserved to be treated the way she had by Francesca, by him, or his mother when she was alive. He was, however, grateful that he had an opportunity to apologize to her for all the wrong he'd done, but that was before the shooting. As he listened to her voicemail, his heart went out toward her. She was especially close to her parents, and all Stiles could hope was for Robert to help her through this terrible time.

Stiles drove the remaining hours without stopping. He passed the hours away by listening to his playlist and thinking over all the things that had happened both recently and in the past. He found himself becoming somewhat depressed as he reflected on his life. As he approached the sign that welcomed him to Houston, he smiled slightly and exhaled. It felt good to be back in Houston, far away from the perils of what he left behind in Memphis.

He exhaled again when he turned into his neighborhood. Tapping the remote, and pulling up into his garage, Stiles remained in the car for a few minutes before getting out and going inside. He had no rhyme or reason to why he remained in the car; he just sat there until his spirit nudged him.

Several minutes later, he got out of his car and went inside the house, which looked and smelled fresh and clean. It was good to be able to rely on his weekly housekeeper to keep everything in tiptop shape even while he was out of town. He went to his bedroom and sat his luggage down by the closet. Before he called

Kareena to let her know he had made it back, he decided he would take a shower and change clothes.

After he finished showering and getting dressed, he sat down on the sofa in his man cave, turned the television on, and mindlessly began flipping through the hundreds of mostly useless stations. He found himself nodding off, but his phone rang and jerked him out of his sleepy state. He looked at the phone. It was Brian, one of the deacons from church who had also become a good friend.

"What's up, man?" Stiles said when he answered.

"Hey, there Pastor Graham, my friend. I was just checking on you, bro. I know you said you were heading back this way in a few days. What's your status?"

"Actually, I just got back. I left out earlier today. I'm about to go get a bite to eat and then come back home and chill. How have things been while I've been gone?"

"Everything is good. No worries. But we missed you, man. Nothing like hearing you deliver that word up in the pulpit. You know what I mean."

Stiles chuckled, glad to know that he was missed but that things had gone relatively smooth in his absence. He was thankful that he had a great group of people surrounding him who supported his endeavors and understood his flaws, that is the flaws he allowed them to see.

"Glad to hear that. I plan to check out the game tomorrow. Call me if you wanna hang out," Stiles said to Brian.

"Okay, cool. Well, go get you something to eat. I'll talk to ya later."

The men ended their call and Stiles immediately called Kareena. She insisted on coming to pick him up rather than him driving since he'd just made the eight hour drive from Memphis.

"How's your appetite now?" Kareena asked when she arrived at Stiles' house.

"I'm starving. Haven't had a bite to eat since I left Memphis, and that was only a slice of toast and a banana."

"Okay, then what do you say we go to Lucille's. It's on this end of the city so it shouldn't take us long to get there."

"Sounds good to me. You know it's one of my favorite restaurants, and it's dinner time, too."

"Yeah, which means you can get the whole fried chicken, mac and cheese, and those smoked greens you like."

"That's what I'm talking about," Stiles said excitedly. "Let's get outta here."

Along the drive, Kareena caught him up with the various meetings she attended at the church, about attendance in his absence and the lighthearted gossip she always seemed to hear.

Upon arriving at Lucille's, they parked and went inside the busy establishment known for its delicious food. Even though there was a forty minute wait, they decided that it would be well worth the wait to be seated.

Time quickly passed as they chatted and laughed. When they were called for their table, they already knew what they would order.

"I missed you," Kareena confessed while they ate.

Stiles hoped his face didn't display the emotions of hearing Kareena tell him that she missed him. It wasn't like she hadn't said it before, but this time her facial expression and the tone in which she said it, seemed to convey something far deeper. He didn't know if he was just imagining it, but felt that he wasn't.

Reaching across the table, he said, "I missed you too," and tenderly grasped her hand. He gently caressed her fingers and looked into her eyes. "You're beautiful, Kareena."

Kareena blushed. This time she couldn't hide it. "Thank you, Stiles, but where did that come from?"

"It's the truth. You're a beautiful woman inside and out."

"Wow, I don't know what to say."

"No need to say a thing. I just wanted to tell you that. Life is so short. It seems I keep getting reminded of that. I never expected to have to bury my sister and brother-in-law. I mean, I don't know what to pray for anymore," he said sadly. "I'm so messed up inside, so I guess seeing you here, looking at you, hearing your laughter, it just makes me know how blessed I am to be able to call you my friend." He continued to caress her fingers.

Kareena eyed him with deep sympathy to the point she felt like crying, but didn't. "I have no words to say, except that God is in control. That's all we can ever say. As far as us being friends, I'm always going to be here for you. You have brought so much to Full of Grace Ministries. I know my father would be proud of you. I know I am and so is the rest of my family. You are an amazing person, Stiles, and I don't know why you've had to deal with so much pain in your life. But you're a strong man and you are going to be fine."

Stiles stared at her, gazing deep into her eyes. "What do you say we finish this feast of food," he chuckled lightly, hoping she didn't detect the rapid beats of his heart.

‡

"Lucille's never disappoints," Kareena said as they arrived back at Stiles' house.

"Yeah, I'm stuffed. I'll have this for lunch tomorrow," he said, picking up the bag of food he had left from his meal. "And thanks for buying. The next meal is on me, for sure."

"I wanted to buy it. Think of it as a welcome home meal." She giggled.

"Hey, why don't you come inside and have a cup of coffee with me, unless you have other plans for the rest of the evening."

"I don't have other plans. I'll come in for a few minutes but you know I've never been a coffee drinker."

"Oh, yea, but I have soda, tea, wine, water."

"Okay. You don't have to twist my arm."

They went inside and Kareena took a seat on the sofa.

"What would you like?"

"Umm, a glass of wine would be nice. On second thought, I'll have a soda. I don't want to drink and drive."

"I don't think one glass of wine would impair you to the point that you can't drive, but if it does, I have two extra bedrooms. It's your choice. Come on in the kitchen and pick out the soda you want. I have several kinds, I'm not a huge soda drinker so I don't know which one to recommend. The housekeeper keeps the cabinet stocked, not me."

"You're so spoiled," Kareena said, laughing. "You know what?"

"What?" replied Stiles.

"I changed my mind again. I think I *will* have that glass of wine. Do you have red?"

"Sure, I prefer red, too."

Shelia E. Bell

Stiles went to the refrigerator and retrieved an unopened bottle of red wine.

"Hey, will you get the wine glasses from out of that cabinet over there," he asked, pointing to the cabinet.

"Ahh, so we're doing this big, huh. Wine glasses and all. I liiike." Kareena giggled again while walking to the cabinet and retrieving two glasses.

Stiles retrieved the wine corkscrew from the cabinet drawer next to the fridge. He opened the bottle of wine and turned around only to bump directly into Kareena who had simultaneously walked up without him noticing. Wine spilled out and onto her dress and on his shirt.

"Dang, I'm sorry. I didn't see you, Kareena." He grabbed a paper towel quickly from the island and began wiping the front of her dress.

"It's okay. I shouldn't have walked up behind you. I should have said something." She blamed herself.

He continued to wipe the wet wine stain nervously until Kareena stopped him, grabbed hold of his hand, and held it next to her bosom.

They looked at each other. Stiles studied her loose wisps of curly thick black hair and her button brown eyes. Sudden silence filled the kitchen. The only sound that could possibly be heard was the pounding of their own heartbeats.

He tried to kiss her but got a cheek and a slow move backward. He didn't know why he wasn't deterred by her move, but he wasn't. Instead he bent down and lightly kissed her lips. This time she didn't turn away. Instead, in return, standing on tiptoes, she embraced him and placed her arms solid around his neck. She felt her knees weaken as the pressure of his lips increased.

The blood began to pound in her temples, and she momentarily stiffened, but still no words were spoken between them. When Stiles pulled back and looked at her, she was powerless to resist, caught up in her own emotions.

"I missed you so much," he said hungrily as he devoured her lips again. He swooped her trembling frame up in his arms and carried her toward his room.

At first Kareena tried to protest, but her feelings were too far gone, so she relaxed in his arms as they continued to kiss. Though she had never admitted to Stiles that she was in love with him, somehow she believed he knew. She prayed that what she was about to let happen again would not ruin her relationship with Stiles but most of all with God. She didn't want to give in to the desires of her flesh, but her heart said otherwise — she listened to her heart.

23

*Before you can see the light, you have to deal
with the darkness.* Unknown

When Hezekiah returned to the pulpit, his messages
were full of fire and brimstone. His anger toward Pastor
had only intensified since he told him weeks ago that he
wanted him out of Holy Rock. He hadn't seen or heard
from the old man since then, and he was more than glad.
Perhaps, in another day, at another time, when he was a
younger man, he could have accepted and forgiven his
father. But too much time had passed and Hezekiah had
seen his share of some tumultuous times in his life. Had
he known years ago that Pastor was his father, maybe he
would have taken a different path other than winding up
in prison and taking his wife along with him. His son had
paid for his sinful acts and ended up following in
Hezekiah's footsteps. The only difference between him
and Khalil was he didn't get hooked on drugs like his son.

Thoughts of Pastor and the relationship they might
have had if the old man had chosen to be in his life,
mentally and emotionally tormented Hezekiah.
Intensifying his pain was the knowledge that Pastor
adopted his brother, Stiles, and chose him to be his son.
What hurt so badly was the fact that Margaret insisted
that Pastor knew about him all along, but not once did he
try to find out where he was. Pastor tried to convince him
that Margaret wasn't telling the truth, but Hezekiah didn't
believe a word that came out of the old preacher's mouth.

As if she could read his mind, Fancy curled up next to
her husband in the bed. "Honey, you have to let go of all
this worry and anger. So much has happened to make you

stressed, and it's not good for you. You know you already have high blood pressure and stress is not good."

"I hear ya, and I keep telling you that I'm straight. I got rid of my main stress - Chauncey Graham…and his son. The only other thing on my mind is that oldest son of ours."

"Well, I certainly agree with you on that. That witch, Detria, is my age. What could she possibly want with our Khalil? And knowing that she cheated on Stiles and had a baby with his best friend is despicable. There's something about those Grahams that brings out the worst in people, I'm telling you," Fancy added.

"The best thing is not to pressure Khalil to stop seeing her because that's only going to drive him that much farther into her arms. We could mess up the good relationship we have with him, you know."

"I hear ya, baby, but I don't know if I can keep quiet. I know she's no good, and messing with a kid as young as Khalil proves it."

"At the end of the day, he's a grown man, he's moved into his own space, and we have to let him make his own choices and his own mistakes. We can give him advice, which we do, and we can be there for him if and when he needs us. But that's it."

Fancy snuggled in closer to her husband, but her arms were folded. She was still quite upset and she had to find some way to make Khalil see that Detria was no good for him.

"So what's up with Xavier?"

"What do you mean? There's nothing up with Xavier that I know of," Fancy replied. "He's doing well in school, and when he's home, like always, he keeps mostly to himself. He's usually in his room reading, playing video games or on his computer or phone, like most teens these days."

"I told you I want you to monitor that. It's not good for these young people to keep their eyes glued to a computer screen all the time. Too much to see on there and too much trouble. He and I haven't talked much, but I've been so busy and so much has gone on that I haven't had the time. I guess I need to make some time to spend with him to see where his head is at. Does he even have a girlfriend? The only person I see him around is Raymone, and I've told to watch that because that boy is questionable."

"Oh, Hezekiah, please. Questionable how? Raymone is a nice, mannerable young man. He's smart and quiet just like Xavier. They're into those games. Xavier is not girl crazy like Khalil. Anyway, you should be glad that you don't have to worry about him running from one girl to the next. Those young girls at Holy Rock Upper School, and at the church, are always throwing themselves at both of our sons."

"That's what I'm talking about. And you're telling me that Xavier isn't interested in any of them? I haven't ever seen him at church even talking to a girl. Right now, he's upstairs with that boy. If he isn't over here then Xavier is at his house."

"That's because they're best friends, Hezekiah. You've had your share of best friends and so have I. Anyway, Xavier is fine, so please don't start making something out of nothing. God knows we've gone through enough lately. I don't think I can take too much more. Khalil and that cradle robber are enough to worry about."

Hezekiah looked at his phone then got up and started putting his clothes on.

"Where are you going?" Fancy asked." "Please don't tell me you have to go make a visit tonight."

"That was a text from Minister Eddie. I have to go to the hospital. Sister Riley has taken a turn for the worse."

"Why can't he go?"

Hezekiah looked at Fancy and partially rolled his eyes in his head. "Are you for real?"

"I'm just saying, I don't understand why they can't make more of the visits."

"Didn't you hear me say that Sister Riley is not doing well. Good, Lord, Fancy. You know that Sister Riley is one of our long time, faithful, tithe paying members. If she wants me there, then I'm going to be there."

Fancy sighed an exasperating sigh. "Then let me get dressed and I'll go with you."

"No, you lay your pretty little head right here. I'll be back as soon as I can. I just need to meet with the family, say a prayer, and I'll come back to you." He finished getting dressed then kissed Fancy and left.

Hezekiah dialed a number as he stepped outside. "Hey, I have to make a hospital run and then I'll be on my way. But I can't stay long tonight."

"Okay, just get here as soon as you can. I miss you, baby," Detria told him.

Detria and Hezekiah had been secretly seeing each other for almost a year. The condo he leased was specifically for their sizzling romantic rendezvous. Before Margaret came and went on her rampage, they met at least once a week, more if Hezekiah managed to get away. This would be the first time they'd seen each other since before the massacre and Detria couldn't wait.

Hezekiah phoned Minister Eddie and told him to meet him at Baptist Hospital. That way Hezekiah could say a prayer for Sister Riley and leave Minister Eddie at the hospital to minister to the family. Sister Riley was ninety-one years old and had Alzheimer's. She wasn't expected to be around much longer, but only God knew that for certain.

Hezekiah followed his well thought out plan and then headed to his condo after spending an hour at the hospital. He laughed when he thought about Stiles. Life was funny. Here he was smashing his brother's ex. Who would have thought. He could see Pastor and Stiles now. They would have a field day about this if they found out that Detria was his mistress. But at this point, Hezekiah's only concern was Fancy. He loved her and he didn't want to hurt her, but he had needs that one woman just couldn't fulfill. He'd always had a woman on the side and never in all the years he and Fancy had been together had she ever acted like she suspected him to be anything other than faithful. He always said that as long as the playa, whether it be the woman or the man, could keep everything right at home, then there was nothing to worry about. So he went out of his way to keep Fancy satisfied in all areas and made sure that whatever she wanted, he got it or did it.

Detria and every woman before her, had to understand that he was not about to leave his wife or break up his happy home life. He treated his women well but he wanted them to understand that he wasn't about falling in love or having kids with them. If they could roll with him according to his rules, then there would be no problem. The moment he noticed, or thought he noticed, that the woman was falling too hard for him or pressuring him to leave his wife, then Hezekiah immediately walked.

As for Detria, she was a different caliber. He was pissed, highly pissed, when Khalil showed up with her at his birthday dinner, but under the circumstances, he couldn't say anything or do anything about it. Later the following day, Detria explained that she didn't know Khalil was his son. She'd never seen his kids because Hezekiah demanded his privacy.

Fancy didn't care much for Detria because when she was Holy Rock's first lady, Fancy had seen Detria and Skip exchange some questionable touching with each other. Fancy never said a word about what she'd seen to Stiles or Hezekiah. She didn't want to be the one that destroyed a happy home or spread gossip about the First Lady. It turned out that Fancy didn't have to do or say a thing because Detria wrecked her own home life and marriage. It came out in the open that Detria and Skip were enthralled in an affair. Detria got pregnant by him and things went downhill from there in Detria and Stiles' marriage.

Hezekiah, much like Skip, found it impossible to ward off Detria's sexual flirtations. He had taken it upon himself to go visit Detria after the accident. He was strictly there to pray with her and help her deal with the loss of her and Stiles baby girl.

When her lover and baby daddy married his other girlfriend, Detria almost lost it. She called Hezekiah and asked if he would come pray with her. That day led to many other days and within a matter of a few months their praying sessions had turned into rumbling between the sheet sessions and they had been seeing each other since.

Lying in the bed next to Detria, Hezekiah brought up his son again. "I can't tell you not to see anyone else besides me, but I can tell you that I don't like that you're seeing my son. For Christ sakes, Detria, he's a boy. And how can you be with me and with him?"

"I told you that I am not having sex with him, Hezekiah. It's not like that between me and Khalil; we're just friends. I talk to him about girls and stuff that an older woman can tell him. He listens to me. You should be glad. At least I'm a distraction from all those hot little girls at the church itching to put a baby on him and ruin his life."

"I still don't like it. It's too close to home."

"Oh, are you jealous?" Detria said, kissing him on his smooth chest and using her leg to run up and down his leg

Hezekiah sat up in the bed. "I don't do jealous, you know that. That's why we've lasted this long. You do your thing and I don't interfere with that as long as you give me my time. I don't have time for jealousy or getting bent out of shape about who you're seeing. I have a wife and I've told you, I'm not leaving her."

"Who said anything about you leaving Fancy? I'm just saying that you're right about me seeing who I want to see. I'm not married so I can do as I please with who I please, and that means if I want to have an intimate relationship with your son, then I can do that too. Either you deal with it or you don't. Your choice."

"Oh, so now you're saying that you and Khalil do have an intimate relationship. I thought you just said that you're like a mentor to him, which I know is a bunch of rubbish." Hezekiah laughed. "Go for it, darling." His eyes roamed over her figure, taking in her nakedness. "He'll never be able to make you feel the way I do. Remember that."

"And you remember this." Drawing her face to his, she pressed her open lips to his.

"Detria," Hezekiah called her name softly between kisses.

Detria basked in the knowledge of the power she had over him *and* his son.

His eyes were as dark and powerful as he was and Detria was captivated by them. She stared back with longing in her own eyes for him. Her heart fluttered wildly as his hands masterfully explored the soft lines of her back, her waist, her hips.

She tingled as he said her name. Her pulse quickened and the thought of being next to him, of him desiring her, made her feel good. She gave in to the searing need for him that had been put on hold for weeks.

After their lovemaking session, Hezekiah showered and got ready to leave.

"You staying here tonight or are you going home?" he asked.

"I think I'll spend the night here. I can't move," she said in a teasing tone.

Hezekiah smiled. "I'll call you later. I may be able to get out tomorrow. I'll let you know for sure."

He walked out of the bedroom and into the living room. Suddenly, without forewarning, he stumbled and everything around him began to go black. His head felt like it was about to explode. He tried to steady himself, but the more he reached out for something, anything to grab hold to, the more he could sense that he was spiraling down...down...down until somewhere in his mind he heard a loud, almost sickening thud before total blackness settled upon him.

Detria heard a loud thud. "Hezekiah. Honey, what are you doing in there?" she called. No answer. She called out again, no answer. She jumped out of the bed and ran out of the room, only to find Hezekiah sprawled in the hallway semi-conscious.

"Hezekiah, baby, what's wrong?" Detria asked as she tried to use her one good arm to cradle him.

Hezekiah's eyes rolled up in his head and foam came from his mouth as he tried to speak. His words were like a baby's, unintelligible and garbled.

Detria saw his phone on his side and jerked it from its holder. She dialed 9-1-1. "Operator, I need an ambulance at 322 Main Drive and I need it now!"

24

All I want in life is for this pain to seem purposeful.
Elizabeth Wortzel

Josie opened the microwave to put in a cup of water to make herself some dandelion tea.

"Pastor, your dinner is still in the microwave," Josie said. "You have to eat something. You need to keep up your energy. If you don't, you're going to make yourself sick," she scolded.

"Can't eat if I'm not hungry."

"You're letting what Hezekiah did send you into this deep depression. But I keep telling you that you need to pray about it and let it go. God will work everything out. He always has and he always does. I'm not telling you anything you don't know."

"I'm tired. I'm tired of fighting the devil. I'm getting too old. I've messed up too much in my life. I have to pay for what I've done, for the people whose lives I've ruined, for turning my back on my own flesh and blood, my only real son."

"Pay for the lives you've ruined? I'm here to let you know, you don't have that much power. And who hasn't messed up? Tell me one person that hasn't regretted doing something, not doing something, saying something they shouldn't have or not saying something they should have, including me. We're not perfect. The Bible says we all have sinned and fallen short. You know that as well as I do."

Pastor didn't respond.

"You can at least try to engage in conversation. Come on, now," Josie said, her concern making a statement in her voice.

"I'm sorry. And you're right; none of us are perfect. But I'm not talking about everybody; I'm talking about me. I need you, Lord," Pastor shifted his conversation to the spiritual realm. "I can't keep going through this. I need you to heal this situation. Heal this family. Heal my wounds, Father God."

"That's right, call on the good Lord." Josie walked over to her husband and placed a hand on his shoulder. "He's the only one who can bring you out of this funk. I can't begin to tell you that I know how you feel. So much has happened to you and to this family. It's been traumatizing, to say the least. But I know you, Chauncey. You're a man of faith. People come to you for counsel, so now it's time for you to use your own words of wisdom and advice."

Pastor turned to face his wife, reaching out and pulling her by the waist to himself. He hugged on her and then kissed her.

"I love you," Josie said and kissed him back.

"I love you, too. You know, I've been thinking about Rena. I wonder how she's doing. She refused to talk to me when we went up there to the Jackson's memorial service."

"Have you tried calling her since then?"

"Once, but of course she didn't answer."

"Why don't you send her a card with a message or try calling her again. She's hurting just like we are. She lost both of her parents so tragically. It was all so senseless."

"Yes, it was senseless. I still can't wrap my mind around any of it."

"I'm sure none of us can. But as for Rena, she needs time to heal and to process everything that's happened in her life. I'm just thankful that she has a husband and kids to help her through this. I say just back off and leave her be for now. God has a way of working everything out in his own time."

Pastor eased away from Josie and stood up. "Again, you're right. Everything will be fine. I'm going to go into the family room. It's almost time for *Black-ish* to come on. You joining me?"

Josie gingerly batted her eyes and smiled to herself. *Thank you that healing is on the way, Lord,* she prayed within. "You know I am. I love that show. Let me finish making my tea and I'll warm up your dinner, too."

‡

In her bedroom, Rena laid alone in the darkness. The house was empty. Robert was at work and the kids were at school. As winter gave way to the first day of spring the forecast called for an expected twelve inches of snow. The cold wintry like weather outside was a perfect correlation to the coldness that formed itself around her heart. The pain of having to bury her parents had not subsided. Quite the opposite, she couldn't function, didn't want to care for the kids or her husband, didn't want to go to work or eat. She remained on leave from work, and her primary care physician prescribed her meds for her anxiety and depression, which only enhanced her desire to do nothing but sleep.

She laid in the bed thinking about how much she despised the Grahams. They had brought nothing but misery to her life. Pastor and Stiles even had the audacity to come to Andover for her parents' funeral. How could they have been so bold? Seeing them was like rubbing salt into a fresh, open wound.

Both of the men had called her several times and she rejected their calls and then she blocked their numbers altogether. If she never heard anything else from either of them or about them it would be too soon. As for Francesca, she hadn't wished death on her ex-lover, but Rena found it difficult, almost impossible, to fully grieve for her. Too much hurt had been inflicted and she couldn't find any place in her heart for forgiveness. Instead, she secretly wished that Stiles and Pastor had been in the line of the bullets and not her parents.

When Robert arrived home from work, he entered the room and clicked on the light. He looked at his wife curled up in the bed, her eyes staring off into space.

"Rena," he called but she didn't answer. She didn't even flinch or look around at him. "Rena," he called again. Still no answer.

Robert turned and walked back out of the room. Minutes later, the twins burst into the bedroom.

"Mommy, we got out of school early," one of the twins said.

"Yeah, it's snowing outside. Look," the other twin said, dashing to the window and opening the blinds.

"Close that blind!" Rena bellowed. "No one told you to come in here and touch a thing!"

"But we just wanted to show you the snow."

Rena suddenly felt bad for yelling at her kids without reason. "Look, Mommy's sorry. I'm just tired and the light hurts my eyes. So please just go to your rooms and play. Okay?"

"Yes, ma'am," the both of them said in unison and then jetted out of the room.

"Close the do--," she said but they had disappeared before she could finish the end of her sentence, which forced her to get up and close the door herself.

While climbing back in the bed, she stopped and looked when she saw her reflection in the dresser mirror.

Her hair was all over her head. Dark circles were underneath her eyes, revealing her unspoken pain. Her lips were parched and she looked frail and quite thin.

Robert returned to the room a second time and saw Rena staring at herself in the mirror. "You need to talk to somebody, Rena. Staying in this room, yelling at the kids, not eating and not going to work, is just not good for you or for us."

Anger lit up her eyes. "My parents are dead! And you, you want to waltz up in here and tell me that I need to talk to somebody. You want to chastise me for being hurt. How dare you!" she said as hot tears rolled down her cheeks.

"You know better than that. I would never make light of your parents' deaths. I hurt, too, Rena, and you think the kids don't miss their grandparents. We're all hurting. But we have to go on with our lives, sweetheart. That's all I'm trying to say. You can't spend the rest of your life holed up in a dark room."

"If you don't like it why don't you leave, or better yet, I can leave. I don't have to put up with this. I have enough on me already." She got back in the bed and jerked the covers up around her neck.

Robert shook his head regretfully before turning around and walking back out the room. He tried to understand what his wife was going through, but the longer she acted like this, the harder it became for him to deal with her. The kids were suffering because they wanted their mommy, the mommy they knew and loved. The woman in the bedroom was a totally different person. She was full of anger and rage and Robert didn't know how to help her. He talked to her sister on a couple of occasions but that hadn't helped matters because she seemed far removed from what had occurred. The only advice she could offer Robert was for him to give Rena more time to grieve.

Robert tried to do all that he could to keep his anger in check. He wanted so much for his wife to get better but it seemed with each passing day, she was getting worse. He hoped she wasn't abusing the pills the doctor prescribed. Something had to give. He wasn't saying that he expected her to be one hundred percent better. But seeing that it had now been over two months since the death of her parents he hoped that she would have returned to work and began to try to live her life without them. From what he could see, she was far from moving forward and he knew it wasn't healthy. This was definitely taking a toll on him and the kids.

"Hey, kids," Robert called out as he left his bedroom.

The kids bolted out of their bedrooms at the sound of their father's voice and gathered around him in the hallway.

"Whaddaya say we order pizza for dinner this evening," Robert told the bunch.

"Woohoo," the twins, Rachel and Riana squealed while the older kids, eight-year old Robbie and twelve-year old Isabelle gave each other high fives.

"Order pepperoni and sausage," said Robbie.

"Noooo, cheese," said one of the twins.

"Hold up, let's go downstairs. We don't want to disturb your mother."

"Is Mommy going to eat with us this time?" Riana asked, looking hopeful.

"We'll see. But first, let's go downstairs and decide what kind of pizzas we're going to order."

25

I wanted to tell you all my secrets but you became one of them instead. Unknown

Detria paced across her bedroom floor, her face furrowed with worry. After she called 9-1-1 she waited until paramedics arrived at the condo and watched them whisk Hezekiah away. One of the EMTs asked her if she wanted to ride in the ambulance but she lied and told them she would follow them in her car. There was no way she wanted to take the chance of anyone finding out that she was the one who called 911, and that she was the one he had been with. He would have enough to explain when he got better about why he was at a condo that his wife knew nothing about.

Hezekiah had the condo in Holy Rock's name. He told Detria that if anyone other than the two people who were instrumental in helping him get the condo found out about it, then he would just tell them he leased the condo as a place to escape from all of the hustle and bustle of being a pastor. Fancy would be more than upset with him if she discovered his hideout, but at the end of the day he knew how to settle her down. All he had to do was buy her something expensive, take her on a trip, and make love to her like crazy.

Detria called the hospital to inquire about Hezekiah's condition. "Hello, could you tell me how Hezekiah McCoy is doing please and if he's been put in a room? He was brought in a few hours ago by ambulance."

"May I ask your relationship to the patient, please?" The person on the other end of the line asked.

"I'm...his sister," Detria told the woman.

"Hold on please."

Detria held the line for several minutes before the woman returned to the phone. "I'm sorry ma'am, but we have no patient information on a Hezekiah McCoy."

"That can't be. The ambulance took him to Regional One. I'm sure of it."

"I'm sorry, but we have no Hezekiah McCoy." The woman hung up the phone.

Detria didn't know what to think. She was certain they took him to Regional One. Maybe they transferred him to another hospital. Or maybe... "Oh my God, is Hezekiah dead?" Is that why they have no information?" she cried. "Oh, God, please don't let him be dead." Her knees buckled as she nearly collapsed into the bedroom chair.

She contacted every hospital in Memphis and no one had patient information about a Hezekiah McCoy. After having no luck with her search, she decided to text Khalil. She would see if he said anything about his father and that way she could find out what was going on.

"Hey babe. WYD"

"will call u soon. my dad n hospital," Khalil texted back almost immediately.

"OMG! Hospital? Wat happened?"

"idk. running tests. ttyl."

Detria was relieved that Hezekiah was alive. All she needed to do now was find out what had happened. She didn't know for sure if he had a heart attack, a stroke, or what. When she found him on the floor, he was barely conscious and couldn't talk or move. Had he passed out and hit his head on something when he fell?

Her cell phone rang. She looked at it and immediately pushed the ACCEPT button.

"Who knows you were with him tonight?" the man asked.

"What are you talking about? Who says I was with him at all?"

"Don't play games with me. You're the one who called 9-1-1. Who else did you call?" the man demanded.

"No one, what are you talking about? What's up with you anyway? I don't like the way you're talking to me," she retorted.

"What happened tonight?"

"I already told you, nothing happened. He was getting ready to leave and I heard a loud noise. I jumped up and that's when I found him lying in the hallway. Is he going to be all right?"

"He's conscious. He had a stroke."

"Oh, Lord. How is he? And what hospital is he at? When I called Regional One they said they didn't have a Hezekiah McCoy and neither did the other hospitals."

"Good to know that privacy feature is in effect. But to answer your question, right now he can barely talk and he's paralyzed on his left side. I don't think he remembers what happened," George told her. "But that may not be permanent. Could just be the initial reaction to the stroke. Don't know if there's brain damage yet or not."

"I just thank God he's alive."

"Yeah, you got that right. I get paid to know where he is and who he's with, especially when it involves him running around with the likes of females like you, so you should be glad he's okay."

"I don't know how to take that, George."

"Take it like this; if he's okay, you're okay, but if I find out you said a word to anyone, you'll be sorry. The First Lady is already asking questions. He was supposed to be visiting one of the members at Baptist Hospital. She wants to know where he was and who he was with."

"I don't have anything to do with that so don't threaten me, George."

George didn't react to her words. Instead he said, "I'll call you back when I have more news. In the meantime, I went to the condo and made sure Pastor McCoy didn't leave anything behind. You lay low and don't breathe a word to your boy toy. And don't barrage him with questions about his father."

"Why would I do that?"

"Let's just say, since you and the pastor have been an item I've come to know you quite well."

"And?" replied Detria

"And, I know what you're capable of, Dee. Now you sit over there in that big fancy mansion of yours and keep your pretty little mouth shut," George said and abruptly ended the call without saying goodbye.

The phone rang again. Detria answered with hesitation. "What do you want, Skip?" she said with irritation.

"Your son is fine, but believe it or not, he misses his mama. Since you don't seem to be interested, I thought I would call and let you know that."

"Oh, how kind of you," she said with bitter sarcasm. "And why are you hassling me? You got him with you. That's what you wanted, so get off my back."

"You're a piece of work. You know that? A real genuine piece of work. You don't bother to get him when it's his time to be with you. You don't call to check on him. It's been months since he stayed at your crib for more than a night and even that was only God knows when. You don't care about your own kid. For God's sake, what's wrong with you?"

"Is this why you called? To try to put me on a guilt trip? And to harass me? Well, I don't have time for it tonight or any other night, Skip. You and your little wifey keep taking care of Elijah and don't call me unless something is wrong with him. You understand? Leave me alone!"

"You don't even want to tell your son goodnight?"

Detria did not respond but abruptly ended the call, got up out of the chair, and went to the bathroom. It had been an exhausting evening and she was tired, sleepy, and hungry. She started a bath, added bubbles, and lit candles around the tub. While her water was running, she buzzed Priscilla on the intercom and asked her to make her a light snack and bring it to her room.

While she bathed, she thought about what was going on at the hospital. George told her that he would call her back, but she doubted that he would. Maybe she should text Khalil, just to ask him how Hezekiah was doing, but changed her mind when she thought about what George had said.

‡

Fancy was practically inconsolable when she arrived at the hospital with her sons and discovered Hezekiah was in critical condition.

"Is he going to be all right?" she asked the nurse at the station.

Khalil and Xavier stood on each side of her for emotional and physical support.

"We'll know more when the doctor comes out. He's still with your husband and they're doing everything they possibly can for him. Please go in the ICU waiting area up the hall," she pointed toward her right, "and I'll come and let you know as soon as I hear something."

"Come on, Mother," Khalil said, leading her in the direction the nurse pointed.

Fancy slowly walked along the hospital corridors with her sons. "I don't know what I'll do if Hezekiah doesn't pull through."

"Mom, don't think like that," Khalil said.

"Yeah, Ma. Dad's going to be good," said Xavier nervously.

They rounded the corner and approached the entrance to the ICU waiting room. Entering the room, they saw two other people plus a familiar face – George.

He stood up when Fancy entered the waiting room.

"First Lady, how are you?" he asked as he walked up to her and embraced her. He held onto her for several seconds.

"What happened to him, George? I know you're always by Hezekiah's side. Was he still at Baptist Hospital when this happened? I don't understand. And if he was at Baptist why did they bring him to Regional One? I'm just so nervous and upset. I don't know what to do," she cried.

George tightened his embrace to provide some comfort to her. "Calm down, First Lady. None of that matters. What matters is that he's here and he's getting the best care possible. And you know Pastor McCoy; he's one tough rascal. He's going to come through this with flying colors. You wait and see."

George stepped back out of the embrace, took her by her hand, and led her to a nearby sofa type chair and she sat down.

"Would you like some coffee or water?" George asked.

Fancy shook her head. "No, thank you. I just want to see my husband. I want to see for myself that he's okay."

"Ma, the nurse said she would let us know when the doctor finishes working with him. I'm sure she's going to keep her word. Now, please, just be cool. Okay?" Khalil wrapped his arm around his mother's shoulder and she laid her head against him.

"Ma, I'll be back."

"Where are you going?" she asked Xavier who was texting and standing to the side of where she was seated.

"Uh, to the bathroom."

"Okay," Fancy responded. "Don't be walking up and down these hospital corridors, Xavier."

"I won't, Ma," he answered without bothering to look at his mother. He continued texting as he walked out of the waiting room. Stepping into the corridor, he walked past the men's bathroom and went to the elevators farther down the hallway.

He pushed the DOWN button, and got on when the doors opened. Once downstairs in the lobby, he went outside and stood in the brisk night air. The moon was full and the air blowing against him sent a slight chill.

"What's up," he said after he dialed the number and Raymone answered.

"You said your dad's in the hospital?"

"Yeah."

"What happened?"

"I don't know. They think he may have had a stroke. The doctors are still working on him. I guess he'll be alright, at least I hope he will. What are you up to?"

"Nothing. Still on this game. How long are you going to be at the hospital?"

"I don't know. Probably until they tell my mom something. Anyway, I'll hit you back when I hear something. I told my mom I was going to the bathroom. I don't want her to send a squad after me. You know whudda mean?"

"Yeah, I hear ya. Text me and let me know what's up."

"Fa sho. Talk to you later." Xavier ended the call and put the phone in his pocket before turning to go back into the building.

"Hey, good looking," someone suddenly said.

Xavier looked up and saw an equally handsome young man who looked to be a few years older than him. Still shy and reserved about his sexuality, Xavier grew nervous and disregarded the guy. This was not the first time that another man had openly flirted with him. Xavier didn't understand it. Could other men or people detect he was gay? If so, how? He heard about gaydar or gay detectors where some people had the ability, or so they said, to tell just by looking at another person whether that person was gay or not. He was not openly flamboyant but was reserved and kept to himself. For that guy or any other guy to feel like they could call him good looking or ask for his number, made him a little uneasy. He wondered if his brother suspected anything or his mother and father for that matter. Maybe they did but chose not to say anything. He arrived back at the elevator and returned to the waiting room. His brother and George were still there. Khalil's head was buried in his phone.

"Where's Mom?" Xavier asked.

"The nurse came and took her to see Dad."

"How is he?"

"I don't know. They still haven't said."

"No need to worry. He's going to be fine," George assured the boys. "Pastor McCoy would want you to look after your mother, make sure she's okay, and to pray."

Khalil nodded in agreement and returned to texting. `"Still at hospital. Dad in critical condition."`

`"I'm so sorry to hear that. u know what happened yet?"`

`"stroke."`

`"u want me to come to the hospital to be with u?"` Detria texted back.

`"I'm good. hit u up when I lve here."`

`"K. I'll say a prayer."`

Three seventeen a.m. Detria's doorbell rang in response to an exchange of text messages between her and Khalil.

`"Can I come ovr?"` he'd texted.

`"Yes,"` she had replied. *Prayer answered*, she thought as she closed the text and smiled.

Detria gave herself a touch up of the body parts and hair and now, forty-five minutes later, she shimmied to the front door to greet Khalil.

"Detria, is everything all right? Did I hear the doorbell?" Priscilla asked, standing inside her bedroom door, arms folded, and in her PJs.

"Ummm, can't believe she woke up," Detria mumbled to herself. "Yes, sorry to wake you, Priscilla. I have a guest coming."

"At three o'clock in the morning? Are you sure?"

Detria gave Priscilla an eyebrow shifting, stay-in-your-lane type of look.

Priscilla shrugged her shoulders, tucked her lips. "Goodnight," she replied and disappeared behind her door.

26

Being sick feels like you're wearing someone else's glasses. Megan Boyle

After a combined month long stay in the hospital and a rehab facility, Hezekiah was discharged but remained unable to walk and talk. He was paralyzed on his left side and his speech was unintelligible. He had a long recovery ahead of him. Doctors informed Fancy that only time would tell if he would get better and be able to walk or talk again.

A CNA came daily to help Fancy take care of him plus several women from Holy Rock volunteered to come assist her as well. Fancy was still a private person so she made sure George had each woman, unbeknownst to them, thoroughly checked out before she allowed them to come into her home. A physical therapist, speech therapist, and occupational therapist came to the house three times a week and once a week Hezekiah was taken to the hospital for therapy.

Fancy was the stand by your man type of woman but Hezekiah's illness was beginning to take a physical and mental toll on her. She was used to him being in charge and running things, but she knew that he would want her to step up her game to make sure things continued to run smoothly and without problems at home and at Holy Rock. She, and others, thought of her as being smart and ambitious. She was responsible for several successful ministries at Holy Rock, starting with the Marriage Ministry and the Youth and Young Adult Ministry. That's why she was happy that Khalil wanted to be part of the Y&YA Ministry. Like his mother, he fit in easily and prospered in his position.

Fancy began to talk to herself. When she sat with Hezekiah and saw the sometimes helpless look on his face or the disturbing grunts and struggles to speak, she regained her inner strength, prayed, and then decided that she would reclaim her office at Holy Rock—effective immediately. This was an opportunity for her to step up her game and show his staff and the congregation that Hezekiah had a strong first lady behind him.

Pastor and Stiles had contacted her on more than one occasion to inquire about Hezekiah's health. She shared little with them. If Hezekiah didn't want anything to do with them when he was in good health, surely she wasn't going to let them disrupt him while he was trying to regain his health. Pastor wanted to come to visit him, but Fancy denied him. There was no way she would take the chance of making Hezekiah upset. She told Pastor that he was recuperating fine, but she would rather he keep his distance.

Fancy spent at least four hours a day at Holy Rock. Everything there was to learn, she set out to learn it. Holy Rock finances, church bills, staff duties, salaries, and responsibilities, vendors, whatever was connected to the successful operation of Holy Rock, she was determined to learn about it. When Hezekiah fully recovered, she wanted him to be proud of what she had done.

What made her even more grateful was that her sons, both of them, but especially Khalil were right by her side, supporting her all the way. Khalil often accompanied her to staff meetings, outside engagements with vendors, going over reports, the whole kit and caboodle. He was game. Because of him, the youth ministry was growing by leaps and bounds and for now it seemed everything he and his mother touched, prospered.

Shelia E. Bell

As week after week continued to pass, George grew increasingly on edge. He had become accustomed to his side *bonuses* from Hezekiah. He watched from the sidelines but with a perfect view, at Fancy and the way she handled Hezekiah's affairs. It led him to believe that she might already know that he and Hezekiah had an arrangement. From being around the couple, George surmised that Fancy McCoy was the only person Hezekiah trusted. It was time to enlighten her about him and her husband's arrangements, because, like Hezekiah, Fancy had just as much to lose if he told everything he knew about their past, Hezekiah's hands in Holy Rock's cookie jar, his mistress, and of course, their gay son.

Fancy sat in Hezekiah's office scanning and reading over tons of computer files. As his power of attorney, she insisted that she be given access to his personal computer at Holy Rock. Reluctantly, the IT department gave her his login information. Hezekiah maintained at least an eighty-five percent paperless office. She reviewed bank statements, grants, and paid special note to the love offering and tithers *aka* high rollers of Holy Rock. Time to resurrect her experience about church administration and finance. The more she studied the records, the more she was drawn to look closer. Something was missing. Not being one to give up easily, she continued to dig.

She spent time every evening, when she got home, talking to Hezekiah about what she did every day at Holy Rock. She asked him questions about many of the things she found in his office and on his computer. Though he couldn't speak, he could nod or shake his head and grunt. His answers most often were strained, with a pleading look in his dark eyes. He would sometimes manage to get a word out, but ninety nine percent of the time, it was darn right impossible to understand him.

One evening, at home, after a relatively unusually short, uneventful day spent at Holy Rock, she stood inside their master closet sorting through items of clothing that she wanted the housekeeper to have sent out for dry cleaning. She pulled out a few of her clothes and then proceeded going through Hezekiah's things. She felt in his pockets to make sure wads of tissue, loose change, or any other items were not stuffed inside. Sure enough, two pair of suit pants had tissue inside, an indication of Hezekiah's ongoing occasional sinus problems. As she removed a suit coat off its hanger, she heard a jingling sound and immediately threw the coat down on the floor and hopped back because the sound reminded her of a rattlesnake. She laughed at herself for being so over dramatic and scary. Picking up the jacket, a set of keys fell onto the floor, the obvious culprit of the strange noise.

Looking at the keys, she toyed with them in her hand. They did not look familiar. After gathering the clothes and putting them inside a bag for the housekeeper, she laid the keys on the nearby chest of drawers. When she went to sit with Hezekiah, she would take them with her to see if he could give her an indication as to what they went to.

Taking the keys and showing them to Hezekiah ended up being another worthless cause because he could tell her nothing. She noticed a glimmer of frustration in his eyes when she showed them to him. He did nod his head up and down when she asked him if he recognized the keys. She asked him if the keys went to a particular desk or box at Holy Rock, he shook his head no. After a series of questions to determine what the keys went to, she gave up as her own frustration mounted.

She exhaled. "Don't worry, baby," she said, patting him on his hand and leaving the keys on the bed. "It's no big deal. If something needs to be unlocked or checked, it'll just have to wait until you're all better. Maybe this will be a small incentive for you to keep improving so you can get back to your pastoral duties, and your husband duties, too," she said, smiling sheepishly.

Hezekiah nodded, grunted, and moved anxiously in the hospital bed.

"Okay, okay. I didn't mean to get you all aroused, settle down there," she continued flirtatiously. She stood up and kissed him on his lips, and squeezed his hand. "I'm going to go check on dinner. We're going to have one of your favorites – spaghetti and meatballs. I'll be back later, sweetheart."

When Fancy attempted to leave, Hezekiah grunted again and again. The more he tried to talk the more agitated he became when nothing came from his lips.

"What is it, Hezekiah? Are you in pain?"

"Unn." Hezekiah shook his head from side to side, this time with a little force.

Fancy's expression took on a serious and concerned look. She removed her phone from her pant pocket and looked at the time. Then she looked at the sheet the nurses used to track Hezekiah's meds and the times they'd been administered.

"I see you haven't had your anxiety meds for the evening."

Hezekiah looked angry as his brows furrowed and he pounded his good hand on the bed.

"It's okay, baby. I'll give you one now." She went into the small dorm like refrigerator that was set up in his room, and pulled out a pint of bottled water. She got his pills off the nightstand and took two from the bottle. "Here, take these," she said but Hezekiah turned his head.

"Hezekiah, come on. You don't have to lay up here feeling anxious and in pain. Now, come on. Take them," she insisted. "If you don't take your meds I'm going to be forced to have the nurses give it to you a shot or intravenously. I know you don't want that."

Hezekiah relented and did as he was told, hoping that it would make her leave him alone.

"Now, get some rest." She picked up the remote from off the bed and flipped the channel to TBN, then laid it back where he could reach it. "I'll be back later with your dinner. I love you," she said, then turned to exit the guest room that she had set up specifically to accommodate her husband and his needs.

Hezekiah looked down and to his right and saw the keys lying right by his good hand. He managed to get them and push them in the trash can next to his bed. *God, heal me,* he said in his mind. *Deliver me from this paralyzed body. I have too much left to do and too many skeletons I need to keep from coming out.*

Living in a state such as he was made Hezekiah all the more anxious about his life and future. So many thoughts raced through his mind while lying helplessly in that bed, but he had no way of communicating his needs and wants. With everything that had happened in his life over the past months, he felt drained. Maybe it would be better if he just gave up the ghost and left this world of trouble all behind. But how could he even do that when he couldn't move or speak? Even if he wanted to commit suicide, he couldn't. Was this what life for him was destined to be? Hezekiah cried and a flurry of tears poured down his cheeks.

He pretty much knew everything that was going on at Holy Rock, well everything that Fancy told him. George had come to see him on several occasions and each time all he ever talked about was getting paid. Hezekiah realized that the man was not concerned about him or his well-being in the least. It was all about the money for George. Not that it surprised Hezekiah, because George was ready to destroy his life if he didn't pay him what he demanded. It would mean nothing to him if Hezekiah died.

One thing Hezekiah was proud of was the fact that Fancy and Khalil were determined to keep hold of the reigns of Holy Rock. Listening to Fancy sharing with him the details of what was going on at the church, who was doing what, and going so far as to show him reports and data about the church meant more than they would ever realize. He just hoped that Fancy didn't dig too deep and find out that he was pocketing tens of thousands of dollars from the church. And those keys Fancy found. That was another source of contention because if she found out what they went to, it would lead to his demise. Somehow, someway he had to regain his movement and his speech. He told himself to work even harder with the therapists. He needed a breakthrough in his health soon and real soon before the walls of lies and deceit came tumbling down.

27

Three things cannot long stay hidden: the sun, the moon and the truth. Buddha

"Mrs. McCoy," the housekeeper said, reaching inside her apron pocket, and pulling out a set of keys. "I found these in Pastor McCoy's trashcan when I was cleaning." She passed the keys to Fancy.

"Thank you, Marcela, I must have unknowingly dropped them in there yesterday. I'm glad you found them!" She accepted the keys and continued walking out the door.

Fancy called Khalil on her cell phone when she got inside her car. "Honey, what time are you going to be at the church?"

"I should be there no later than ten. I have a stop to make and then I'm headed that way. Do you need me to bring you anything?" he asked.

"No, I'm good. I'm just leaving the house myself. Xavier left for school about an hour ago. I started to ride in with him, but you know how that goes."

"Yeah, he doesn't want to be seen in that car with anybody but his friends, or should I say friend, as in the one and only Raymone." Khalil chuckled into the phone.

"You're laughing, but that concerns me."

Khalil continued to laugh. "Why, Ma? 'Cause he's not riding girls around?"

"Well, not exactly, but then again, yes. I'm in agreement with your father now. I don't know why he has to hang around with that boy all the time. He used to have girlfriends when he was younger but now that he's almost eighteen, he rarely, if ever mentions girls."

Shelia E. Bell

"Just 'cause you don't see him with a girl doesn't mean he isn't messing around with 'em. He probably just hasn't stumbled across one that he really likes. I know they're all over him at church, so you know they're all over him at school."

Fancy sighed. "I guess. And you're right, it's probably a good thing he loves his books and that video game more than these hot tail girls running around. I do not want to be a grandmother. I'm too young. And that brings me to you." Fancy stopped at the traffic light.

"Uhhh, what about me?"

"I hope you aren't still infatuated with Detria Graham. That woman is bad news."

"I don't agree with you on that. She's actually a nice woman. I like her. I like her a lot, Ma." Khalil didn't tell his mother that he had just left from dropping Detria off at her house. She had spent the night with him at his apartment, where he hardly ever spent time anymore. Most evenings, after he left Holy Rock, he would head straight to Dee's house. She spoiled him in all kinds of ways but her specialty was providing him his favorite dishes and never ending, mind blowing sex. He was definitely smitten by her.

"You need to be careful, son. I mean you have a lot to offer and well, I would like to see you with someone your own age."

"Yeah, someone like Tori, huh?"

"Not necessarily Tori, but a nice, bright, ambitious young lady. Someone who has her head on straight and who won't be with you because of who you are."

"I can say that Dee is not with me because of my money or my ambition. She has plenty of money and she doesn't need ambition." Khalil laughed.

186

"Just be smart. The same way you're smart when it comes to helping me handle your father's affairs and the state of Holy Rock, then that's how smart you have to be when dealing with someone like Detria."

"Yes, Mother. I gotcha."

"You betta. I'll see you in a few," Fancy said and ended the call.

Fancy arrived to her office at Holy Rock, locked her purse inside the file cabinet, checked her emails, and then went to Hezekiah's office.

"First Lady," George said, approaching her in the hall

"Oh, good morning, George. How's it going?"

"How is Pastor McCoy this morning?"

"He's doing well, but I can tell that he's still frustrated about being bound to that bed and unable to walk and talk. I'm praying every day that he gets better and back to the Hezekiah I know. I hate to see him this way, you know."

"I know. I can't imagine being in his shoes. And I'm sure he misses being here at Holy Rock and doing what he loves. This brings me to ask you something I really feel awkward about. But, well, you're the only person I can come to since Pastor McCoy is out of commission."

Fancy stopped walking and looked at George seriously. "What is it? Hold up; let's go to Hezekiah's office so we can talk in private," she said, looking around the parameters of the hallway.

"Okay," George answered and they continued to walk to his office.

She unlocked the door and they entered the office.

"Okay, have a seat and tell me what's on your mind," she said and took a seat herself behind Hezekiah's desk.

"I don't know how to say this other than to say it. I've been working on a confidential matter for quite some time for Pastor McCoy."

"What kind of confidential matter?" Fancy looked at him strangely. *What has Hezekiah gotten himself into?* she thought

"I guess I need to cut to the chase."

"Yeah, you do. So tell me, what kind of confidential matter?

George's phone rang. He looked at it and then stood up from his chair. "I'll talk to you another time. I have to take care of something," he said and quickly exited the office.

Fancy watched as George left. She would let Hezekiah know when she got home that he needed to find a way to tell her what was going on with George, but for now, she was more interested in what the keys she found unlocked.

She pulled them from out of her purse and began to see if they worked with any of the cabinets in Hezekiah's office. They didn't. She looked around his office, tried to see if they fit his desk drawers, looked underneath his desk for any secret compartments, and inside the cabinet in the meeting room adjacent to his office. None of the keys fit. She even tried the doors to the meeting room and his office but again none of the keys worked.

After exhausting her efforts to find out what the keys went to, she gave up and started looking through files on his computer again.

Khalil arrived shortly after and she told him what George had said to her.

"It's probably nothing to be concerned about. You know how Dad is. He always has something going on. If it was that important to George, he wouldn't have gotten up and left."

"I don't know. Maybe you're right. Anyway, I'm going to mention it to your father."

"Why mention it to him when he can't tell you anything, Ma? Let him concentrate on getting better instead of worrying about something he can do nothing about and neither can we. Now, if George comes back to you and tells you what he's talking about, address the issue then. Until then, let it go."

"You are wise beyond your years. You're so much like your father. I'm so proud of you," Fancy said.

"We're in this thing together, Ma. That's what families do. They stick together."

28

"All women are natural born espionage agents."
E. Cantor

It was minutes away from eleven o'clock. The house was quiet. Hezekiah was asleep and Xavier was at Raymone's house. Fancy tossed and turned in her bed. Thoughts ran through her mind about George and Hezekiah. Despite what Khalil suggested, she just couldn't get out of her mind what George could have been talking about. She sat up in her bed and then thought about the keys. She put on her robe and went downstairs to Hezekiah's office. She took the keys with her. Maybe they went to something in his office.

Sitting at his desk, she pulled the drawers to his desk out one by one. Nothing hidden. She was about to give up and then pulled out the last drawer, accidentally pulling it off its railing. The drawer and its contents spilled to the floor. She leaned down to pick everything up, but then like one of those spy movies she'd seen one too many of, she got out of the chair and got down on her knees. She started looking at his desk to see if there were any secret compartments, but there were none. Next, she got up and walked over to where the shelves of books were. Maybe there was a hidden compartment somewhere among the rows of books. She pushed books in, aside, and pulled a few out but again there was nothing. For the next few minutes, she stood in the center of the office and looked. Her mind was racing with curiosity.

Finally, she walked back to Hezekiah's desk, sat down in the chair, and proceeded to put the drawer back on its hinges. She pushed the drawer in and it stopped. She pushed harder, but the drawer wouldn't go all the way in. She stuck her hand in the back of the space and felt something hard. She tried pulling whatever it was out, but she couldn't. She opened the middle desk drawer and retrieved a mini flashlight Hezekiah kept inside. Turning it on, she looked to see what was keeping the drawer from going all the way back in. When she did, she saw a small steel box about the size of one of those boxes that holds a new cell phone. How had she missed seeing it? She messed with it until she was able to pull it out. When she pulled it out she saw that it was an unusually small lock box. She picked up the set of keys from off the desk to see if any of the keys would open the box. Bingo, the second key she tried unlocked the box.

Fancy looked inside. Strangely, all the box contained was three keys identical to the keys on the set she had in her possession, a micro SD card and a cell phone. Unlike her set of keys, the keys in the box were labeled. One was labeled SB, one was labeled DC, and the third was labeled POB. Looking at the box again, she flipped it over. Taped to the bottom of it was another key which was a duplicate of the key that unlocked the box. "What are you up to, Hezekiah?" she questioned aloud. She turned on the phone and it was fully charged. It looked like a burner phone, one of those phones shady business guys use to carry out shady deals. She scrolled through the phone Contacts which consisted of a mere five names and numbers. Her eyes bulged when George's name appeared. The other contact was the name of an apartment complex. Under that contact in the address section was the address 3201 River Circle. She did a Google search and it turned out that it was a luxury complex located in downtown Memphis. Why on earth would Hezekiah have the name of a condo on his phone and why George's number? Could this somehow have

191

anything to do with whatever George started to talk to her about. Another contact was Bank of America. Underneath it were two numbers that looked similar to bank account numbers. Under that same contact were the words Safe Box followed by a five digit number. Fancy took a screenshot of it and continued scrolling to the next contact. This one had the initials DG. She did the same thing; took a screenshot of it with her phone. The last contact said P.O.B. In the note section under the contact were the words Post Office followed by a four digit number, which she also took a screenshot of. She then went back and did a screenshot on George's number and the apartment listing.

Next, she took the micro card, inserted it into the appropriate slot on the computer, and waited for it to open. What she saw next caused her to become physically sick to the point she wanted to throw up. Hot tears poured from her eyes and traveled down her cheeks. A wave of nausea formed in the pit of her belly as she saw several sexually explicit pictures of her husband with, of all people, Detria Graham. There were also several short videos of the couple that made Fancy's head swim.

To see Hezekiah with Detria Graham, was unbearable. The love of her life, the man who's butt she wiped, the man who was the reason she served six years in prison, the man she adored and worshipped. How could he do this to her? And how could he do it with the likes of Detria Graham, the same nasty tramp who was sexing her son!

She nervously scrambled for her cell phone. "Khalil, I need you to come over here now," she cried into the phone.

"Ma, what is it? Something wrong with Dad?" Khalil asked, surprised to hear from his mother at this time of night.

"Your father's okay. Just get here as soon as you can."

"Okay. I'm on the way."

"What's wrong?" Detria asked when Khalil moved her away from underneath the curve of his arm. He jumped up out of the bed and began to hurriedly get dressed.

"I don't know. That was my mom. She needs me at the house now."

"I'll go with you," Detria said.

"No, you stay here. I don't know what's going on and until I find out, then you hang back. I'll call or text you."

He stepped into his shoes, grabbed his keys and wallet off the dresser, and left out of his apartment like he was superman going to rescue a damsel in distress.

He drove as fast as he could. When he arrived about ten minutes later, Khalil used his key to unlock the door to his parents' house and rushed inside.

"Ma, Ma, where are you?" he yelled and dashed toward the bedroom where his father was. He opened the door and saw Hezekiah was asleep. He closed up the door and turned to run upstairs, but he was intercepted by his mother.

"Shhh, quiet," she ordered under her breath. "You don't want to wake your father. Come on," she said and walked to Hezekiah's office.

"What's wrong with you, Ma?"

"I found these in one of your father's suit pockets." She showed him the set of keys as they entered the office.

"Okay, and? Please don't tell me you brought me over here because of some keys." Khalil began to look and sound irritated at his mother.

"This is what one of the keys unlocked." She showed him the lock box. "Inside was this stuff." She showed him the duplicate keys, the cell phone, and the micro card. She continued talking and Khalil continued standing, hands folded, waiting on a valid reason for his mother getting him out of the bed with Detria to bring him here.

"See for yourself. Oh, God, Khalil, I'm so hurt. I don't know what to do."

Khalil walked over and stood behind Fancy who was sitting back in front of the computer. His eyes must have been, had to have been playing tricks on him. Surely he wasn't seeing his father and Detria on a video making love. The video was short but it was followed by three more videos of Hezekiah and Detria in the throes of making love. There were also a dozen or more pictures of the couple too.

"I tried to tell you that little tramp was no good for you. And she's messing with my husband, too. Oh, God, how could Hezekiah do something like this? And why would he keep such disgusting photos and videos?"

Out of nowhere, Khalil slammed a fist down on the oak desk, startling Fancy to the point she let out a yelp as if she'd been struck.

"That son-of-a—....I'm going to kill 'em!" He stormed out of the office.

Fancy jumped up and ran after him. "Khalil, baby, stop." Fancy pulled on his shirttail trying to keep him at bay, but Khalil was no match for her petite, 120 pound frame.

Khalil disregarded her, and burst into his father's room.

Hezekiah woke up to loud noises, hollering and cursing. When he saw Khalil burst into the room, he didn't know what to think. He knew something was seriously wrong, but what? Had something happened to Fancy or Xavier? What reason would Khalil be at the house this time of night and in such a state.

Fancy screamed, cried, and pleaded but to no avail. Khalil dashed over to his father and began choking him. "You lying, cheating, dog. You deserve to die. How could you," he spat and screamed while Fancy pulled and pulled on him.

"Khalil, stop it! Stop it, Khalil! You're going to kill him!" Fancy screamed.

Suddenly, Xavier appeared. With all the commotion, no one heard him enter the house. "What are you doing?" he yelled and charged toward his brother, forcing him off of Hezekiah.

Hezekiah began grunting, shaking his head, and the word no pushed forth out of his mouth. Tears came down his eyes as he continued to say, "Nooo," louder and louder. His eyes bulged as he coughed to regain his breath.

"What's wrong with you? Are you crazy?" Xavier yelled. "Ma," he said looking at his distraught mother. "Are you all right?"

"You're going to pay for hurting my mother. I don't give two cents about that side chick of yours. Tricks like her can be bought a dime a dozen. But you cheated on my mother with her? For how long, Dad?"

Xavier stood by his father's bedside speechless, trying to understand what Khalil could be talking about and what had just went down.

"If it's the last thing I do, I'm going to make you pay. You think lying up in this bed is hard, well you ain't seen nothing yet!" Khalil left out of the room. Xavier ran after his brother, unaware that much like his dad, his skeletons might soon come out of hiding, too.

29

Love grows where trust is laid and love dies where trust is betrayed. Tigress Luv

"Get your clothes on and get out!" Khalil demanded. An Uber driver is waiting outside for you."

"An Uber? Baby, what's wrong? What happened at your parent's to get you so upset? Is Hezekiah...I mean is your father all right?"

"Did you hear me? I said get your clothes on and get out."

Detria got out of the bed and began getting dressed. "I wish you would just tell me what's going on. What have I done? What happened? Baby, please."

"What happened? Is that what you asked me?"

"Yes, tell me. What's got you so upset?"

"Upset? Me? I'm not upset, Dee. I'm done. I mean, you were good in bed, good with the gifts, but that's all you're good for."

Detria slipped each foot into her shoes, straightened her skirt and blouse and continued pleading with Khalil to tell her what happened to cause him to behave this way.

"Who do you think you are talking to me like this? It's obvious something or someone has made you mad, but don't come up in here talking crazy to me."

"I'll talk to you any way I please. You're nothing to me."

"Is that so? Mighty funny you weren't saying that earlier when we were between the sheets."

"You're nothing but sloppy seconds. Why didn't you tell me that you were my father's hoe?"

Detria was appalled. She hauled off and slapped Khalil as hard as she could. *How did Khalil find out? Hezekiah couldn't have told him; he can't talk. And Hezekiah wouldn't have said anything even if he could talk.*

"Don't you ever call me that! And as far as me and your father, you must be hallucinating because I don't know what you're talking about."

Rubbing his face from where Detria had slapped him, Khalil said, "For the last time, I'm telling you to get out of my apartment, you lying tramp. If I ever see your face again, I swear you'll be sorry. Now get out!" He grabbed hold of Dee by her elbow and practically drug her to the door. He opened the door and as soon as she stepped on the other side, he slammed it closed in her face.

Next, he went to his office, sat down at his computer, and pulled the micro card out of his pocket. He'd had went back into his father's office before he left and retrieved the micro card. He bypassed the pictures and videos and opened another folder on the card. It was an excel file that showed a long list of withdrawals from Holy Rock's account, deposits into a Bank of America account, and dates and times of money given to none other than George, his father's number one security guy. What was this all about? Was his father stealing from his own church? And why would his father be paying George under the table when he was already paid a salary? He continued to look through the files. He surmised that George had something on his father. Could it be that George knew about his father's affair with Detria and threatened to tell Fancy unless Hezekiah paid him? Or maybe George knew about his parents' background. Khalil knew there had to be something major because there was no way his dad would set out big bucks like this if there wasn't something George had on him. He would find out and he didn't care what it was, George wasn't getting another dime.

Khalil looked for his cell phone then realized he must have left it in his car. He got up, went back out to his car, and sure enough it was on the passenger's seat. He got his cell phone and saw that he'd missed several calls from his mother and a text from his brother.

"Ma, don't worry. I'm good, just handling some things. talk to u in the morning. try to get some rest," he typed, texting her so she hopefully wouldn't worry and think that he'd gone and done something stupid. He texted Xavier back too and told him not to be so quick to take sides until he found out the whole deal about what was going on.

"hit u up ltr lil bro n letchu kno whuzzup." He ended his text to Xavier.

Next, Khalil called George. He didn't care how late it was. He was waking this dude up to see what in the heck was up between him and his father.

‡

George sat outside on his deck nursing his fourth glass of whiskey and smoking a cigarette. His wife didn't like him smoking period, but since he'd been a smoker since he was eleven years old, he wasn't about to quit, nor did he desire to quit. Smoking relaxed him and mixed with his favorite brown liquor, he could relax even more.

When his cell phone rung, he was surprised to see Khalil McCoy's name and number. Something must have happened to Hezekiah. He hoped the fool hadn't killed over without paying him what he owed him.

198

"Hello, Khalil."

"Meet me in my office at Holy Rock first thing tomorrow morning, seven a.m." Khalil said with apparent anger in his tone. He didn't give George time to respond. He said what he had to say and ended the call

"Hello? Hello?" George repeated then realized the call had ended. He called Khalil back thinking that the call had dropped, but Khalil didn't answer. He called a second time. Same thing. No answer.

George's text notifier chimed. It was from Khalil.

"7 a.m." the text said. "And don't be late."

Who the heck does that little punk think he is talking to me like that? George thought and poured himself another shot of whisky and lit another cigarette. *His pappy better be having his boy pay me my money.*

‡

Fancy left Hezekiah in the room alone with Xavier. She couldn't stand the sight of him. Stroke or no stroke, her sympathy for him was null after what she'd seen. She went to her room and cried buckets of tears until she couldn't cry anymore. Her eyes were swollen almost shut. To find out the way she did that Hezekiah betrayed her hurt worse than hearing the judge sentence her to prison all those years ago. She and Hezekiah had been through so much together, but one thing she never worried about was him cheating. He may have done some awful undercover stuff, but cheating, no one could ever have made her believe that he would turn to another woman to satisfy his needs. Not when they had such a good marriage and sex life. She lay in the bed, thinking about if she had missed any signs that would have warned her

Shelia E. Bell

about his infidelity but she could think of none. How long
had he been messing around with Detria, of all women?
What else could he be hiding? What else was on that
card? Fancy wanted answers to the string of questions
going through her mind. With Hezekiah being unable to
talk, it was going to be hard to find out anything.

The pictures and video replayed in her mind. A light
knock on the door momentarily sucked her away from the
disgusting thoughts.

"Come in," she said softly.

"Ma." Xavier entered the room. "I was just checking
on ya. How are you?"

"Not good." A fresh batch of tears starting streaming
from her red eyes.

Xavier walked over to the side of her bed and sat
down next to his mother. "Don't cry, Ma. Please don't
cry."

"I can't help it. I can't believe he would do me like
this. I've been nothing but good to your father. I thought
what we had no one could ever come between."

Xavier felt horrible. He didn't know what to say to his
mother, especially not knowing the details of what
happened earlier while he was gone. "Ma, what did Dad
do? What happened?"

Fancy spared no details. She was hurt and at this
point, she wanted Hezekiah to hurt too. The best way to
do that was to let his sons know what he'd done to their
mother. Granted, she didn't want them to hurt Hezekiah,
at least not while the man was already on his sick bed.
Had he been healthy, she would have welcomed them
beating his lying, cowardly, cheating tail.

Like Khalil, hearing what his father had done,
angered Xavier. Blood may be thicker than water, but
when it came to choosing between his father and mother,

his mother would win every time, hands down. No wonder his brother exploded the way he did. He, too, had a mind to go back downstairs and yank his father out of his hospital bed and give him a whooping like he'd never forget. But no matter what, Hezekiah was his father. No way could he muster up enough strength or courage to hit him. There were other ways to hurt him that weren't physical. Xavier had a strange feeling that his brother would find a way to do just that, and when Khalil did, Xavier knew that he would join forces with him to make Hezekiah McCoy pay for what he'd done.

30

The soul always knows what to do to heal itself; the challenge is to silence the mind. C. Myss

Lying in her bed day after day, night after night, Rena thought about what Robert had said. Her family needed her, and she needed them. She thought she heard her parents' voices telling her to get up and move forward with her life. She began to pray and cry out to God, something she hadn't been able to do for some time.

Slowly she began to show signs of returning to her former self and she soon decided that it was time that she returned to work. With Robert's full support, prayers from friends and their church, she was finding the resolve to cope with her new normal. It took a while but she was almost back to the lovely, happy, vivacious woman, wife, and mother that Robert had fallen in love with. It was still a struggle, but for the most part, she had determined within herself that she would make it through and come out much stronger for it. Her parents would have wanted that for her. They would have wanted her to be happy again.

Rena, Robert and the kids burst inside their house laughing and talking about the movie they'd just returned from seeing.

"We had fun," one of the kids said.

"Yeah, I want to see it again," another one said.

The other two kids joined in the conversation talking about how great the movie was. For Robert, it was good to see that his family was getting back on track.

"I love you," Robert said and snuggled up against his wife, kissing her on the earlobe. "I hope you had a good time tonight."

Rena turned and looked at him. She placed her hands around his neck. "Yes, I had a wonderful time. And I love you Robert Becton. I love you with all of my heart," she said and kissed him lightly on the lips.

"Ewww," said Isabelle. "Why do you guys always have to kiss?" she said before turning and running out of the kitchen.

Robert and Rena laughed and Robert kissed her again, picked her up, and twirled her around.

"Ahhh," Rena screamed and laughed.

It felt good to laugh again, to smile again, to enjoy her family again. Granted, she longed for her parents to be there, to share in all of the love and laughter they used to enjoy with their grandkids. That was the sad thing about it. Rena felt that they all had been stripped from the life of what would have been if they were still alive. But all of that had been taken away by a lunatic and this further confirmed for her that it was all connected to the Grahams. She would never ever in life want to see them again or be near Stiles or Pastor. They were the epitome of evil to her and she hoped that they were feeling ten times the pain and anguish she felt.

"Let's get the kids in bed so we can have a little playtime," Robert teased as he held Rena by the waist and walked with her to the family room where the kids had gathered.

"I've been praying for Hezekiah night and day. I know God to be a healer. He healed me again and again. He'll do the same for my son."

"Pastor, I'm praying too. We have been in a storm for quite some time. Not just us, but our friends and family.

Have you talked to Fancy anymore or anybody from Holy Rock?"

"Fancy won't answer my calls anymore, but almost every day one or more of me and Josie's friends from the church call. It's a blessing to have people who care about you."

"Yes, sir, it is. I've texted her a few times myself and like you, she doesn't respond." Stiles looked over his shoulder and smiled at Kareena.

Stiles was saddened when he heard about Hezekiah. They were just two years apart in age, and Stiles felt it could as easily have been him who had the stroke and not his brother. He was thankful that his health was not in question. He prayed for a speedy healing for him. It didn't matter that the two of them didn't see eye to eye. They were still brothers through blood and in Christ, believing in the same God, and living in their pastoral calling. There was no room for grudges or wishing ill against another person.

"Pastor, have you still been visiting other churches?"

"Yes, Josie and I worship somewhere every Sunday. No one can stop that. I've been talking to her and praying about going back to Holy Rock. And it's not because Hezekiah isn't in the pulpit. It's because God reminded me that no one can put me out of the church, and surely not the church that I founded. I can be voted out of the pulpit, but no way will I be booted out of the building. He can hate me all he wants, but he'll have to take me to court."

"I agree and I support you." Stiles was one hundred percent in his father's corner. Hezekiah may be the senior pastor but what right did he have to ban him from attending Holy Rock. Pastor said Hezekiah would have to take him to court, but Stiles laughed at that. He had no legal legs to stand on against Pastor. He was prepared to help the only man he'd known as father, the man who adopted him, cared for him, and loved him. He would not turn his back on him. "Listen, I'm glad you called. It's always a blessing to hear from you."

"Same here, son, and Josie says hello."

"Hi, Josie," Stiles said loudly into the phone, and laughed.

"Well, I guess I'll talk to you later. Josie and I are about to watch our show."

Stiles laughed. He admired the relationship Pastor and Josie had in each other. They were each other's support systems, and most of all each other's best friend. He used to want that same thing, but not anymore. Falling in love was the last thing on his agenda. It wasn't even on his bucket list.

"Gnite and God bless you. Bye."

"Okay, Pastor. Gnite."

Stiles pushed the END button, laid his phone down on the table next to him, and then turned and looked at Kareena.

"Sorry about that. I didn't mean to be rude."

"Rude? Be for real. That was your father. What's rude about talking to him?"

"Another reason I'm crazy about you," Stiles said.

Kareena smiled and eased back a little so she could look into his eyes. "Crazy about me? Uhhh, where did that come from?"

"What do you mean where did that come from?"

"I'm not going to play games with you, so just forget it."

"I like you. You know that, Kareena. You also know that I'm not looking for a First Lady. Been there done that."

"Duh, from the man who just said out of nowhere that you're crazy about me. Have I displayed anything more than friendship toward you? Let me answer that for ya; no I have not. I think I can clearly remember that, uh, it was you who pushed the envelope. And I'm not stupid; I understand that it was all physical. A man is a man is a man. I get it."

"It's not like that and it wasn't like that. You're beautiful, Kareena. Any man would be a fool not to be attracted to you. And I hope you don't regret what happened between us. Okay, we got caught up in our flesh, but by the same token we're two adults, two consenting adults. If you feel that what we did was wrong, was sinful, then that's between you and God. But me, I don't feel guilty or sorry."

"You're so far out in left field. How many times have we had this same conversation? Once? Twice? A hundred? Maybe not the exact words but definitely the same meaning. So can we not do this again tonight?"

"I'm with you, so are you ready for me to order that pizza?"

"Yeah, the movie will be on in less than an hour, and I'm hungry."

"Okay, I'm on it," Stiles said. Why had his heart betrayed him to the point that he couldn't take the chance again to love or be in a relationship. He could easily justify his feelings for Kareena because she was so easy to love, but it had been proven to him twice that love wasn't enough. And for him, he didn't believe that the third time would be the charm.

31

Things come apart so easily when they've been held together with lies. Dorothy Allison

Khalil sat in front of George in his father's office. It was time he found out everything about the business dealings George and his father had going on. Xavier sat in the chair across from him. Khalil had called him the night before to meet him at his apartment. He shared everything about his findings with him. Just because Xavier was only seventeen, Khalil felt it was still important for him to know the family business. He didn't want him blindsided like his father had blindsided his mother and them. Plus, Xavier was a genius when it came to stuff like the spreadsheets and reports on the micro card.

George looked like he was ready to lock both of them up and throw away the key. But his days of playing cop were over so he resigned himself to listening so he could see just how much these youngsters knew about the dealings of their scoundrel father.

"I know my father was paying you an astronomical amount of money on the side, plus you're on Holy Rock's payroll. I don't want to hear anything but the truth. No run around bull crap either. I've been through every line of those transactions. I know when they started but now I want to know why. So what do you and our father have going on?"

"You boys need to stay in your place. The business me and your father have going on is between us. I don't care what you have or what you think you found. Yes, he was paying me, and to be frank about it, I want my money. I haven't received a dime since he had the stroke.

By the way, how is the old boy doing, seeing that you won't allow me to see him anymore. That's messed up."

"We're not here to talk about my father's health. And you're right, he isn't allowed to have visitors. We want to assure that people like you aren't coming to see him. So let's cut the chase. You are *not* going to get another red cent until we know what's going on. My mother is my father's power of attorney, and she is in agreement with us."

George was furious. He bolted up from his chair, placed both palms on the desk, and stared with bloodshot eyes at Khalil then Xavier.

"Listen to me you little punks. Unlike your father, you don't know who you're dealing with. Because he knew that I could ruin his life and everything he thinks he has in this farce of a church, he paid me and he paid me well. And if you have any sense in that drug filled brain of yours, boy you'll keep paying me."

"You won't be getting a darn thing, George," Fancy said, boldly stepping into the office and slamming the door behind her.

"Ahhh, so looks like I have the whole McCoy clan here. That makes things even better. "Fancy, you sure you want to do this?"

"I'm more than sure. And that's not all I'm going to do. Effective immediately, you're no longer head of Security. You're fired. I want you out of here."

George laughed. "You don't know what you're doing. Do you know the garbage I have on your husband and this family? You couldn't possibly know because if you did, the only meeting we would be having now is the one where you're telling me that you're giving me a bonus! I can send you and that embezzling, cheating hubby of yours back to jail at the drop of a dime, crazy lady. And

208

here's something else you might want to feast your eyes on," he said, pushing a micro card across the desk toward Khalil. "Before you make any decisions, I suggest you take a look at this."

Khalil eyed George suspiciously. Xavier looked and so did Fancy as Khalil slowly placed the card inside the USB port. Some of the same pictures that were on the file Hezekiah had were on George's files. But what they hadn't seen was footage of Hezekiah and Detria talking about Fancy and how Hezekiah wanted out of his marriage. There was also a video where George told Hezekiah that he was from Chicago and that he had found out everything about him and Fancy's criminal background, his son's time in a juvenile detention center and his addiction to heroin."

"So my father was paying you to keep your mouth shut about this? Well, that's even more reason for you to get out of here and never show your face again. My mother, unfortunately, already knows about Detria Graham. And she's not embezzling anything from this church. We've gone through those files and nothing incriminates her. Whatever happens to my father, well that's on him. He's dug his own ditch to fall into," Khalil barked. "So, go right ahead," Khalil warned. "Tell Holy Rock, tell the whole world about it if you choose. It won't make us look bad. It will make *him* look bad, and at this point, none of us cares how much he suffers."

"He can have that tramp," Fancy added. "And you, you can take your blackmail files and stuff it where the sun don't shine."

Xavier remained quiet, taking in everything around him.

Khalil suddenly stopped. The color drained from his face when he opened the last remaining file and several images opened.

"Oh, my God! Noooo, what are you doing?" Fancy screamed as she, Khalil and Xavier looked at sexually explicit pictures of Xavier and Raymone.

Xavier jumped up to run out but Khalil yanked him by his shirt, pulling him back down in his chair. "I got this, bro," Khalil said, maintaining his composure and looking at his embarrassed younger brother.

Fancy sat down in a chair, held her head in her hands, and wept.

"Mother, don't cry. We still have business to tend to," Khalil said, sounding eerily like his father.

"Yeah, you heard him. It's time to talk about a raise," George said, laughing. "That is, unless you want Holy Rock and the rest of the world to know about your little gay son and your cheating, embezzling husband. He's skimmed tens of thousands of dollars from Holy Rock. How do you think he afforded to take you on all of those luxury trips, huh First Lady McCoy?"

"The church pays for that and you know it."

"If you believe that, then you're more naïve than I thought. The church pays him well, but it's never enough for Hezekiah. He always has to have more. You should know that, First Lady. You're not that stupid are you?"

"Leave my mother alone!" Xavier yelled. "Or I swear to..."

"Ohh, so the li'l gay boy has a backbone. Now that's hilarious." George chuckled loudly. "But enough of this. You're wasting my time. Now let's get back to talking about that raise," said George.

"No, actually we've talked long enough. It's time to call the authorities."

"You've got to be kidding me. Do you know who I am? Do you have any idea who I know? And what are you going to accuse me of? Blackmail? You can't prove a thing. I don't care what you think those files show. Remember, I have the masters to everything, and what you think you have is not half of what Hezekiah McCoy had on that card."

"But I bet I can prove that you have child pornography in your possession and let's throw in the exploitation of minors. Those images you have are of sixteen year and a seventeen year old kids. And by the way, how long have you been into underage boys, George?"

George went from gloating to baring the look of a whipped puppy. "What are you talking about?"

"I did a little investigating of my own, George. You see, you're not the only one who knows 'people' as you put it. That's why you took those pictures. And let's just say that the list I have of the boys you've brought to that downtown condo. I don't think I need to say more." Khalil said boldly. "Tell me now, who's got the last laugh, Georgie Boy?"

Khalil didn't flinch. His stony eyed gaze locked in on George. His tone was just as hard. "So, let's get something straight once and for all. I am still my father's son and so is Xavier. I've learned a lot from him. From now on The McCoy boys are running things." He transferred his look toward his brother. "And Xavier, our first order of business is for our father and old Georgie boy here to pay the piper."

Xavier poked out his chest and for the first time, he smiled.

Fancy wiped away her tears with the back of her hands and sat up proudly.

"So, I say, let the games begin, George. Oh, and one more thing you should probably know before your time comes to an end—you're looking at the new senior pastor of Holy Rock. From now on address me as Pastor Khalil McCoy.

COMING JANUARY 2018

"DEM MCCOY BOYS"

Book VII

of

My Son's Wife series

Words from the Author

Some of you might say, "Why all this confusion and drama in the church, of all places? My answer – why not. You see, we are all human beings with spiritual identities that last eternally. Yet, while we exist here in the flesh, in this temporary and physical body, we will mess up, shake up, stir up, even in the midst of us loving up, kissing up, holding up, and speaking up. There is so much negativity going on and so much hurt and pain being caused in this world today and the church is not given a reprieve. But that should be no surprise because the church is made up of flawed people living flawed lives with flawed outcomes. That is why God had to do what He did, which is to redeem us even while we were yet sinners. It is why I am so grateful that when I mess up like the people in the *My Son's Wife* series messed up that I know God, my Spiritual Father that I can petition. He goes before His father and intercedes on my behalf. Then He delivers me, cleans me up, and gives me another chance. He lifts me up and places me back on the bicycle of life and there I go, riding again!

This is My Confession
My name is Shelia Bell. I confess that I am a writer. I am an author. I am God's amazing girl. I confess that I write perfect stores about imperfect people like The McCoys and The Grahams, and guess what? Like Me….and YOU!

Thanks for reading another Shelia Bell novel!

More Titles by Shelia Bell
*Some titles are written under former name of <u>Shelia Lipsey</u>

<u>YA Titles</u>
House of Cars
The Life of Payne
The Lollipop Girls

<u>Novels</u>
Show A Little Love (*out of print*)
Always Now and Forever Love Hurts
Into Each Life
Sinsatiable
What's Blood Got To Do With It?
Only In My Dreams

<u>Series Books</u>

Beautiful Ugly
True Beauty (*sequel to Beautiful Ugly*)

<u>My Son's Wife Series</u>
My Son's Wife
My Son's Ex-Wife: The Aftermath
My Son's Next Wife
My Sister My Momma My Wife
My Wife My Baby…And Him
The McCoys of Holy Rock
Dem McCoy Boys

Adverse City Series
The Real Housewives of Adverse City
The Real Housewives of Adverse City 2

Anthologies
Bended Knees
Weary to Will
Learning to Love Me

Nonfiction
A Christian's Perspective: Journey Through Grief

Contact information
www.sheliaebell.net
sheliawritesbooks@yahoo.com
www.facebook.com/sheliawritesbooks
@sheliaebell (Twitter & Instagram)
@literacyrocks (Instagram)